SURPRISINGLY MATCHED

CATHRYN BROWN

Sienna Bay Press

PO Box 158582

Nashville, Tennessee 37215

www.cathrynbrown.com

Cover designed by Najla Qamber Designs

(www.najlaqamberdesigns.com)

ISBN: 978-1-945527-39-5

Surprisingly Matched/Cathryn Brown. - 1st ed.

❀ Created with Vellum

DEAR READER

Surprisingly Matched takes place near Kenai, Alaska. It's south of Anchorage on the Kenai Peninsula and a favorite destination of locals and visitors alike. I've fished for salmon in rivers not far from Andy's lake house and camped nearby many times.

But it's not as much of a vacation hotspot during the winter, and that's when Samantha finds herself there. March in many places is warm, and spring is upon you. Most of Alaska is still snow-covered.

It may be cold outside, but there are warm hearts in *Surprisingly Matched*. And four cats and a dog liven things up!

I hope you enjoy Andy and Samantha's story.

PROLOGUE

*S*amantha Santoro made notes in the margin about the dog treat recipe she'd tested. *Disaster. Don't try this again.* Then she tossed the notebook on the counter.

Everything lately had been a disaster. With her website catastrophe and sales in a downward spiral, testing new treats had become a waste of time and money, neither of which were in abundant supply.

Gracie, her rescue dog, leaned against her leg. Sam wasn't sure of her pet's breed or breeds, but she had fallen in love with the small black dog at first sight.

"We've got each other, though, don't we, girl?"

Gracie wagged her white-tipped tail.

Sam knew her current problems had an easy solution: fix her website and get orders coming in again. That shouldn't be a problem.

But that hadn't been true so far. She'd had lots of problems.

The phone in her pocket rang, and pulling it out, she saw her marketing expert's photo on the screen. Answering, she said, "Hi, Nathaniel." He had helped grow her business, but she didn't have the income right now to justify any more marketing.

"Samantha, I just tried to check something on your website. Do you realize—"

She let out a breath and closed her eyes. "Yeah, I do. The website designer won't respond to emails or calls." Gracie woofed, and Sam reached down to pet her.

"Why didn't you call me right away? I know people who can help you."

She didn't say what immediately came to mind. *Because I felt like an idiot?*

Nathaniel continued. "If it can't be fixed, you may have to start over." He hesitated. "How much can you spend on a new one?"

A hysterical laugh bubbled up, but she forced it back. She told him an amount, and it was met with silence. "I know that's low."

"Can you increase it?"

"Nathaniel, my website has been this way for at least a month. I couldn't understand why sales had plummeted. Then someone called to order treats for their store and told me they'd tried to order online, but my site didn't work."

She sat on her couch, and Gracie jumped up beside her.

"You had a great new website!"

Sam rubbed her hand over her face. "I know. The designer had gone over and above." And then, he had gotten mad. *I'll never do business with a family friend again.*

"I'm on it. Let me try to get either someone who can fix this or build a new site. But Samantha, that's a tight budget."

She knew that. She'd been trying to find someone on her own for days. Instead of feeling humiliated for being taken advantage of, she should have called Nathaniel first. "Thank you."

"I know a man who might do it as a favor to me."

She wanted to ask if the man knew what he was doing, but Nathaniel anticipated her reply.

"He's the best. You would normally pay many times this amount."

"Thank you." She ended the call.

Gracie snuggled closer. As Sam petted her dog, she decided to move forward with her most dreaded plan. She'd check to see if they'd hire her back at Sassy Seafood. Every time she considered that, though, she could feel her blood pressure rising.

She knew her friend Kelsey could probably step away from prep work in the morning for a quick phone call without upsetting the restaurant's owner, Pieter. She definitely couldn't interrupt a dinner service for anything less than a major earthquake.

"How's everything, Sam? I miss having a friend for a boss."

"I'm considering chef work again." She didn't want to admit she'd failed completely, so she added, "To support my business in these early days."

Sam could hear the happiness when her friend replied. "That would be amazing! The summer tourist season will be here soon, so I'm sure that Pieter will take you back."

Sam pictured being at the stove during a busy dinner service during Anchorage, Alaska's tourist season, and the stress of that image had her putting her hand on her racing heart. On the other end of the phone, she heard whistling that she knew came from the restaurant's owner. It faded away and a door slammed.

ATHRYN BROWN

"Okay, Sam, what's really going on? You said you'd never work in a restaurant again."

Kelsey knew her well. "I've had a setback with my website and therefore my business. I need to bring in money to save it."

"Are you going to call Pieter?"

Sam took a deep breath and let it out slowly. She could do this. "I have one last shot at a website. If that doesn't work out, I'll call him later this week."

"That makes me so happy! I'm jumping up and down beside the Dumpster in the alley."

Sam laughed. Finding a friend in Kelsey had been one of the best parts about working at that restaurant. "Say hello to your husband and son. I'll call you when I know more."

"I hope that's soon."

As Sam tucked the phone in her pocket, she said, "Gracie, things with my business need to change quickly or I'm going to have to work in a restaurant and find a doggy daycare for you."

Gracie would have no way of knowing what that was, but Sam's tone must have made it sound terrible because her dog dropped to the floor and covered her head with her front paws.

CHAPTER ONE

*a*ndy O'Connell kept his eyes on his computer screen as he reached for the phone ringing from beside him on the couch and answered it. "Top Tech."

"I need to ask you about a website."

He peeled his gaze from his work and checked the phone. Nathaniel Montgomery. His brother was married to Nathaniel's sister.

"If you have a second, Andy, could you check out this site?"

He didn't have a second to spare, but he liked Nathaniel and considered him to be family. "What's the address?" Andy's eyes widened in amazement as the website Nathaniel had told him about popped onto his computer. Mutant animals cavorted across the screen.

"Are those supposed to be dogs?"

"Bad, right?

"They are." Andy watched the creatures dance.

"You can see four legs, ears, and a tail."

"On some of them, but not all. You're telling me that this

site belongs to one of your clients and that you recommended the web designer who created it?" Andy regretted his words the moment they came out of his mouth. "I'm sorry, Nathaniel. I shouldn't have worded it that way."

Nathaniel chuckled. "No offense taken. She hired this man all on her own. I suggested to her that she needed a new, more functional website and gave her the names and contact info for several designers including you."

Andy clicked on the *About* button at the top of the page. Nothing happened when he did that or when he clicked anything else. Not only was it an ugly website, but it was also a completely nonfunctional website. "I see a shopping cart, so it looks like she has products even though I can't get to that page right now. If so, this isn't a simple website that I can knock out in a short time."

"She does sell products. She makes dog treats."

"That's the business?"

"Oh, yes. It's a very lucrative business. She uses only high-quality ingredients, and the dogs love them. Our dog Chloe went crazy for them when I brought some home from a meeting with her."

Andy looked over at his orange striped cat, Lucy, who was sound asleep on a chair across from him in the living room. "*Only* dog treats?"

"She seems to be a dog lover. I know that may be hard to imagine for a man with—how many cats do you have now? Three?"

He set his laptop beside him on the couch and rolled his shoulders to relax them. "Three and one more that seems to want to live here. I finally brought her into the house and took her to the vet only to discover that she's expecting kittens. So we're about to go from a four-cat house to a who-knows-how-many cat house."

Nathaniel finally said with a chuckle. "And I thought one dog was a challenge when she adopted me."

A caricature of a gray-haired woman smiled at him from the top of the page. Nathaniel's client must be a sweet old lady who'd been taken to the cleaners over her new website. Andy stared at the screen. "It's kind of mesmerizing."

"So, can you work on the site? Fix it?"

Andy pulled his gaze away from his computer and rubbed a weary hand over his face. "Nathaniel, I would love to help you with this project—"

"That's great!"

"You didn't let me finish the sentence. There was a *but*. I have so many clients right now for new websites and updates to old ones that I'm putting in a lot of hours every day." He closed his eyes for a moment. "Too many hours. Since you're family, I'll add that I've been so busy I didn't have time to go to the family lunch last Saturday. Mom has threatened to make me host this week if I forget to confirm that I'm coming by Friday night."

"I don't doubt she'd do it. The entire family may be on your doorstep next Saturday. It's been a while since we've seen your house, so Jemma, our daughter, and I may have to come." A second's pause was followed with, "Um, now, about this website. She's a very *nice* lady."

Andy chuckled. "It wouldn't matter if she was kind and sweet and the most beautiful woman I'd ever seen. Well, those things might help."

Nathaniel laughed. "If you're sure?"

"I don't have any other option. Not today." He'd stopped working on his laptop long enough that Lucy got up, jumped on the sofa, and curled up on his lap. He petted her, something he hadn't done as much as he should lately because of his workload. "Once I get through this batch of jobs, maybe in a couple weeks, things will look better."

Nathaniel muttered what sounded like, "That will probably be too late." But then he said more loudly, "Thank you for looking at it."

∼

A few days after Samantha talked to Nathaniel about her website, he called her back. This time, he had a recommendation for a web designer. "Contact Top Tech. He's the best."

She'd never heard of that company, but she hadn't heard of most of them. Before she'd contacted five highly rated website design companies this week—only to be quoted a price several times what she could pay—she hadn't heard of them either. "Give me his website's address, and I'll look him up while we talk."

"He doesn't have one."

She must not have heard him correctly. "Someone who designs websites doesn't have one himself? Isn't that how customers find him?"

"He says he has so much business that he doesn't need to generate more. He's a word-of-mouth web designer. But if you'd like to check out other sites he's done, you can go to mine, my wife's, or my brother-in-law's. Each is very different, but you can see that each functions well." He rattled off the domain names and Sam wrote them down.

"But do any of them have a shopping cart?"

"No. But before you argue that those sites don't help you, you need to go over to Playful, an online toy store. He designed their entire website, and it has a very functional shopping cart."

She went there and discovered an adorable site. After clicking around on it, she found it worked perfectly. And Jemma's site sold her design and furniture-flipping services well.

"He's exactly what I need. How do I get in touch with him?"

"I'm emailing that info to you now." Then he became quiet, and she wondered what was going on. "Nathaniel?"

"He's very busy, but I'm hoping it will help that you're my customer."

"Why would that matter, aside from business courtesy?"

"His brother is married to my wife's sister." He quickly added, "But this isn't about family. This is about being the best."

Samantha chewed on her lip. "Can I afford the best?"

"You told me your budget." Nathaniel hesitated before saying, "He's also a good guy. I think that will be fine."

"Is there anything you're not telling me?"

Another pause. "Give him a call and see what he says. I'll talk to you soon."

Staring at her phone after he'd hung up, Sam knew this was it. Her business would have to close in another month or two if she couldn't get a website up and running—and within her budget.

Sensing that something wasn't right, her dog bumped against her leg, then leaned there. Sam petted her on the head. Then she took a deep breath and blew it out slowly before dialing the number Nathaniel had given her. When her call rolled over to a voicemail, she debated about leaving a message and decided against it.

Begging would be hard in a message. She'd call again later.

After lunch, she tried the number again.

A man answered the phone. "Top Tech."

"I'm interested in a website."

"I'm not taking new clients."

Before she could say "Nathaniel sent me," he added, "Sorry," and hung up.

She'd have to create a new website herself. Up to this point, she'd run the business on her own with Nathaniel only helping occasionally with marketing. How hard could it be to build a website?

CHAPTER TWO

*S*amantha put the last box of dog treats on the stack in her storage area. "That looks like it, Gracie. I've done all I can here."

Her dog softly woofed behind her in acknowledgment of her words. Gracie sniffed around the boxes, then sat in front of one labeled "Beefy Bites" and looked up at Samantha with a hopeful expression.

"You want a beef treat? Is that what you're saying?"

Gracie held her gaze.

Laughing, Samantha reached in her pocket and pulled out one of her dog's favorite treats. She held it out, and Gracie gently took it from her hand and gobbled up the squirrel-shaped doggy delight.

"Okay, let's get out of here now. I have to go home to watch another how-to-build-a-website video and try to copy their results."

When her dog followed her out of the unit, Samantha closed the door and put the padlock back on it. Then she fastened Gracie's leash to her collar, and they went out to her SUV.

Her phone rang as she opened the SUV's passenger door for Gracie. Her dog jumped inside and Sam quickly unfastened the leash and closed the door. She took the call without looking to see who it was.

"Hello?"

When no one spoke, she realized she should have answered her phone in a more professional manner.

"Goodness Gracie! How can I help you?"

"We'd like a case each of the Beefy Bites and Chicken Chewies to replenish our inventory. We tried to order through your website and pay online, but it doesn't seem to be working."

Samantha held back a groan. Putting on her brightest smile, which she hoped carried over into her voice, she said, "I'm experiencing a bit of technical trouble right now. I hope to get that sorted out soon. But I am always able to take your order over the phone."

Now in full business mode, Sam pulled a pad of paper from her purse and took the customer's information. She immediately recognized the business's name as belonging to one of her regular customers. The man gave her his credit card number, and Sam promised to ship the order that day.

Gracie was in no danger of overheating on a twenty-five-degree day, so she left her in the vehicle while she jogged back to the storage area and grabbed the two cases of treats her customer had ordered. Having the phone number on the website had been the saving grace—the only saving grace—in her website design debacle.

She made a quick stop at the shipping center to get the boxes on their way to her client in California, then went home. If she didn't get this problem solved soon, she and her sweet black lab were either going to be driving south from Anchorage to Idaho to live with her brother and his family or she'd be back at Sassy Seafood. Both of these were less than ideal.

At home, she fired up her laptop and sat down at her dining room table, which doubled as her desk. Sam pulled up the next video on how to build a website from scratch. At this rate, she suspected she'd have the skills to turn out something that wouldn't send potential customers away in six months to a year. She wished her savings would stretch that far.

She attempted what they explained in the video and came up wanting. The website her sister-in-law Jenny had made for her when she had started her business had been fairly basic, but it had helped her get the publicity she needed early on. Sam had known from the beginning, though, that the site would have to be redone when she wanted to include more products. Jenny didn't have the skills to take it further, and she also had a new baby.

Yesterday's conversation with Nathaniel came to mind. He'd recommended Top Tech. The man on the phone had told her no. Her dad had always said to keep trying. If that man said no over the phone, it didn't mean she'd get a no if she showed up at his place of business. A quick search of the business license database showed that the business's head-quarters was near Kenai, a favorite summer destination for Anchorage dwellers and tourists alike, especially during salmon fishing season. There wasn't much going on in that area in March, though.

She stood. "Gracie, we're going on a road trip!"

It was already the middle of the day, but they'd get down

there before nighttime. She dreaded the drive home in the dark, but she'd be okay. Samantha stuffed her suitcase into the back of her SUV, along with other gear, including ample dog food for several days, in case the pass closed before they could get home. Then she went around her vehicle and opened the passenger door.

"Get in, Gracie. Time to find out if we have a solution to our problem."

Her black dog jumped up and sat on the front seat as she would any other day. Life seemed normal to her.

It wasn't.

A single flake of snow landed on Sam's nose. She brushed it off and scanned the gray, cloudy sky. The forecast included light snow, but owning a four-wheel-drive meant she should be fine no matter what those clouds dropped on her.

After three-hours behind the wheel, with a couple of stops for the human to stretch her legs and the dog to take a potty break, her GPS told her she was getting close. But they weren't anywhere near a town. Of that she was certain. They'd passed the signs for Kenai and kept going.

She slowed down to take a turn off the highway. The road immediately narrowed and deteriorated into an acceptable but not great secondary road with infrequently driven winter road conditions. She followed that for a couple of miles and then took another turn to the left. Road conditions deteriorated even more, and her phone's service bars dropped.

Sam said, "Gracie, I think our GPS has led us astray. Maybe it's poor reception." She frowned. "And this web design company was my last option."

When her GPS stopped working near their destination, she checked the address she'd written down. A few minutes later, she slowed down as she pulled up to a mailbox with those numbers on it. The driveway had been plowed, but it didn't show a lot of use, so she wondered if this even was a business address. Was she about to pull into a homeowner's driveway?

"You're all in, or you're not in at all," Dad's often-said words echoed in her head.

She turned the wheel, and they went down the long drive through woods and finally came to a large, beautiful house with lots of windows and a rustic wood exterior. Sam pulled up and took a deep breath. "This may be the stupidest thing I have ever done." She ruffled Gracie's ears. "You and I are a team, though, and we girls are going to get through this."

So she had two clear options. She could put on her business hat, stand tall, walk up to that door, and knock on it. If it was the wrong door, she would probably be fine. She was pretty much in the middle of nowhere now, though. And she was clearly trespassing since she was parked in someone's driveway, which might annoy the owner. She really didn't want to deal with anybody who was upset.

Then there was the second option: turn tail and run like a chicken.

But that didn't get her anything she needed and sealed the deal on her having to go south to live with her brother or go back to work in a restaurant. She'd almost reached the point where the restaurant work alone wouldn't help enough. Option one was the only choice.

She zipped up her coat and pulled on her knit cap. Then she turned to Gracie. "Don't worry. I'll be right back. I hope I have good news for us when I return."

Gracie woofed. When Sam opened the door, her dog barked louder and tried to follow her.

Sam stopped. Her usually sweet and gentle dog must need to step outside for a moment. Sam clipped on the leash, and Gracie jumped down. Expecting her to wander around and do her business, Sam rehearsed her words to the owner of Top Tech. Instead, Gracie tugged her toward the house and gave another *woof*. Gracie had become a guard dog.

Samantha crunched her way through the snow and ice over to the door. As she raised her hand to knock, she paused inches from the door. "Oh, Sam, just do it."

Gracie woofed again.

"Sit and be quiet."

Gracie sat on the step.

Sam gave a couple of solid raps on the door. Instead of the geeky looking guy with a pocket protector she'd expected to find if she had the right address, a handsome, bearded man with reddish-brown hair stared at her. About her age, he reminded her of someone—a handsome someone —but she couldn't place him.

The man stared at her and said, "Are you lost or hurt?"

Beyond him, she saw a gorgeous home with soaring wood-covered ceilings rising to a peak in the middle and a wall of glass overlooking what was probably a magnificent view. Right now it was all white through those windows, but she could see towering mountains in the distance.

She felt warmth radiating from inside the home, but not from the man. As she opened her mouth to give her rehearsed speech, Gracie barreled into the house, pulling Sam along. They plowed him down as her dog raced forward.

"Sorry!" she cried as she flew by the man, who quickly rose to his feet.

Her dog raced to a sofa with four cats perched on it.

Three of them jumped to the top of the back, but one sat and waited for the four-legged invader to reach it.

"Gracie, stop!"

Her dog slammed her bottom on the wood floor and skidded to a stop, coming to a halt mere inches from the lone cat.

The man had quick reflexes and leaped between Gracie and the cats with his arms out. "Your dog is scaring my cats. Please take it outside!"

"I'm trying. Gracie!" She tugged on the leash, but her dog stayed firmly seated on the floor, eyes locked on the cat, who had moved to where it could see around its owner and seemed unconcerned about the situation. When a cat on the back of the couch gave a single hiss, the calm cat jumped up to join the others on their supposedly safe perch.

Sam tugged on the leash again. This time, Gracie got to her feet and allowed herself to be led to the still open front door and outside with only one glance back at the felines.

On the front step where she'd started, Samantha stared at the snow-dusted wood beneath her feet and struggled to compose herself. *Think: business. You're here to save your business.* She looked up into deep blue eyes. That sense of familiarity struck her again.

"Are you lost?" he asked again.

Get a grip, Sam. You've seen more than one handsome man in your life. "I'm looking for Top Tech. A web design firm. Do you know where I can find them?"

He stared at her without answering. Then he asked, "How did you get this address?"

The reality of the situation became clear. She'd chased down this stranger to ask him to please kindly build her a cheap but amazing website. Embarrassment washed over her.

"The business license is registered to this address. There must be a mistake. I'll leave now. I'm sorry about my dog." She would have offered to pay for any damage to his home, but she couldn't afford to sand his wood floor if Gracie had scratched it up. Her dog hadn't touched anything else.

Andy closed the door on the woman. As soon as he did, he realized that he'd been incredibly rude to her. She'd probably needed a web designer and had thought knocking on his door would be the right thing to do. She hadn't realized his business and home were the same address. With her pink hat and matching bulky winter coat, he had only seen her pretty face and fluffs of blonde hair sticking out around the hat. Her expression as the dog had knocked him to the ground had been cute.

But that dog of hers!

He opened the door to wave her back, but she must have run to her SUV. She'd already turned it around in the driveway and was almost to the road.

His clients came to him through a referral from a marketing expert or previous customer, never from a visit to his home office. Not only had he been rude to her, he'd also insulted whoever had sent her to him.

The last two weeks of work had been so intense that it had even cut into his sleep time. He had to say no to the next person who asked him to touch their website. Too much work and no play had made Andy . . . cranky.

CHAPTER THREE

*S*amantha drove away. When she glanced in her rearview mirror, she was surprised the tires hadn't melted through the snow with all of the heat she was generating. That man!

She gave the accelerator a little too much gas, and the rear of the SUV swished on the road. Easing off the gas, she focused on calming down. Nathaniel had recommended him, so she knew he was a good guy. She needed to appeal to his kind side. He must have one.

"Gracie, we're going back."

When she pushed on the brakes, she immediately knew she'd made a mistake. The glint of sunshine off of ice on the road in front of her made her heart leap into her throat. The tires caught on snow but lost traction when they hit the ice. With the SUV spinning in a circle, she pumped the brakes, but it kept sliding. She tugged a trembling Gracie into her arms and held her close as she braced for impact.

As the SUV dove over the edge of the road toward the snowbank, a twisting, metallic sound stopped her vehicle with a jolt. If she had to guess, she'd say that a very large rock had just made this not-great day infinitely worse.

The shining light in all of it was that they hadn't hit hard enough to set off the airbag, because that might have not only injured her but also her dog. Sam looked around the landscape and saw that the nothingness she'd driven past on her way in hadn't changed. She was quite a distance from the highway and help from a passing car. A quick check on her phone showed that the cell service was exactly as it had been before—nonexistent.

She could walk to the highway and hope someone safe stopped to help her. Or she could walk about the same distance to that man's house. He may have been grouchy, but he hadn't seemed violent.

Besides, there was no way anyone in Alaska would turn away a freezing stranger, so she gathered together what she and Gracie needed. She wrapped her dog in her winter jacket and put her little winter boots on. She'd bought them to protect her paws from sharp ice, but now she hoped they'd also keep her feet warmer for their long walk.

If she'd planned for this, she would've been wearing a much warmer coat, boots, and gloves. She had thought she'd be driving to a business near other businesses, not into the middle of nowhere. In the summer, this would be a happening place, she suspected. Sam grabbed the blanket she always kept across the backseat for Gracie to stretch out on and wrapped it around her shoulders for more warmth.

"Ready, Gracie!" She put as much enthusiasm as she could muster up into her words.

Gracie rested her head on Sam's arm and whimpered.

"I know, girl. I'm scared too."

When she opened the door and the cold air blasted in,

instead of wagging her tail with excitement as she usually would, the dog moved to the other side of the front seat.

Sam stepped to the ground. "Honey, we both have to do this. Let's get going." She held out her arms. Gracie tentatively walked over. Sam picked her up and set her on the snow, then closed and locked the doors out of habit. Everything would be quite safe on this unused road.

And they started on their walk back.

It didn't take very long for her driving gloves to stop delivering much warmth. She could feel the cold working through the soles of her boots. If she was getting cold, Gracie's pads on her feet must be frozen. She scooped the small dog up into her arms, wrapped her in the blanket, and continued on.

The sun dropped lower in the sky, and a new, scarier reality came to her. If she was gauging her distance well, and she usually did, it would be dark quite a while before she arrived at the house. Darkness would fall with a vengeance. Her one light would be the flashlight on her phone; otherwise, it would be pitch dark with only the stars glittering overhead reminding her of the difference between earth and sky.

The good news was that the road was plowed, so as long as she stayed on it, she would be going in the right direction. White snow stretched in all directions off of the soon-to-be-dark road. Disoriented, she walked too near the edge of the roadbed and stepped knee deep in snow.

Gracie whimpered as Sam dragged her feet out of the snow and back on the road. "We're going to be okay." She put as much confidence in those words as she could, hoping they'd help her and Gracie.

Step by step, she moved as quickly as she dared on the

snowy and sometimes icy road. She snuggled Gracie close to her chest like a mother with her child, pulling the blanket snugly around her shivering dog. The sun dropped below the horizon in a fiery ball. The light dimmed and went dark as though someone had snuffed out a candle.

Sam stepped onto a patch of ice and her feet went out from under her. As she fell, she held Gracie upright so she didn't land on her. Sitting on the frozen ground, sorrow swept over her. She'd gone too far for her business, endangering herself and her sweet dog.

"I'm sorry. Gracie."

Her dog lapped her tongue over her cheek and woofed as if to say, "Let's get going!"

"You're right." Sam levered herself to her knees, stood, and continued down the road—in the right direction, she hoped. Light filtered through the dark night and must be from Andy's house. Sam focused on the vision of the house as it became clearer with every step. The light grew brighter, turning from vague glowing into light pouring out of windows.

Gracie shivered in her arms.

Sam snuggled her closer and said, "Honey, we're almost there. We're going to be okay." She tried to walk faster toward her destination, but her motions were slow and unsteady. Hypothermia was setting in. She knew the dangers of it and how her life could end if she didn't get care quickly.

Each step was harder than the one before, but finally, she trudged up his driveway, then up the three steps, which had seemed irrelevant before. She rapped on the door, but made little sound with her gloves on. She struggled to peel off her right glove with her dog in her arms and her hands barely working. When she finally did, she reached up and knocked, then knocked again harder, and again louder still.

The door pulled open, and warmth poured out as she started to fall forward with Gracie in her arms. The man grabbed her and dragged her through the doorway before closing it. Gracie slid out of her arms.

"Help my dog. So cold." Sam's eyes started to close as the warmth sank into her. She tried to say more, but the words barely came out. "Help."

"No, you don't. You're not falling asleep. I'm going to move you closer to the wood stove. And I'm going to go get some blankets."

"Gracie?"

"Your dog is already curled up next to the wood stove. I think she's going to be fine."

Sam gave a single nod and let him help her closer to the warmth. He set her down on a soft rug after pushing aside some kind of furniture. Then a second later—at least it seemed like a second—blankets were draped over her.

It felt so good to be warm. She wanted to take a nap. Rest. She felt his presence next to her and turned in his direction.

"No. Stay still. We need to warm you up gently and not move you until you're feeling better."

Gracie curled up next to her and licked her cheek. Sam laid still as he told her to.

Andy watched his guest from the sofa. His four cats were in an upright, alert position and watching the dog. When she'd come over to her owner and stretched out beside her, Lucy had hissed but hadn't moved. The dog seemed completely oblivious, probably because it was so cold. He picked up the throw from the back of the sofa and covered the dog with it.

He shouldn't leave the woman until she was stable. Andy pulled another blanket out of the hall linen closet and stretched out on the couch. It might be a long night.

CHAPTER FOUR

*S*amantha felt wetness on her cheek and reached up, touching Gracie's nose. When she opened her eyes, it was to a soaring wood-covered ceiling in a place she didn't recognize. She sat up and found that she was wearing the clothes she'd put on yesterday for her business meeting, or at least one she'd hoped to have with Top Tech.

Gracie nudged her, letting her know it was definitely time to go out for her morning bathroom break.

When Samantha rose to her knees, the room started to spin around her. She reached out to the floor to steady herself, then stood slowly. There was a wood stove not far from her. She remembered warmth during the night. A kitchen with wood cabinets lining its walls and a massive island topped with what appeared to be granite dominated one corner of the room. As she turned to her left she found the sofa with a man asleep on it, the man from Top Tech. It all came rushing back to her.

He stretched and opened his eyes, staring up at her. "Are you okay?"

"I think so. I don't remember too much about what happened after I got here. I barely remember walking up the driveway."

He pushed back the blanket that was over him and stood, dislodging four cats. Gracie noticed them and went over to investigate the strange creatures. Hissing ensued.

"Gracie!" Sam said as firmly as she could, and her dog responded by sitting. But Gracie watched the cats as though daring them to do something that would allow her to get up and do her job as protector.

Both Sam and the man tried to speak at the same time.

Sam fell silent, and he said, "Before you say anything, I need to tell you this: I'm sorry I was so nasty yesterday. It's no excuse, but I've been working too many hours. What happened after you left?"

"My SUV hit an icy spot, we spun, and we went into a ditch. I think it's about halfway between here and the highway, so I walked back. Gracie's paws had to have been cold even with her boots on, so I carried her most of the way wrapped in a blanket."

He was a handsome man with reddish-brown hair. When he smiled, she knew why he'd seemed familiar. "Oh my goodness! Andy?"

He stared at her. "Do I know you?"

She pointed at herself. "I'm Lou's sister. Samantha Santoro." She'd come here to ask what turned out to be her brother's college roommate to work on her website. She wouldn't have believed that could be possible if she hadn't experienced it. Truth truly was stranger than fiction.

His jaw dropped and he staggered backward. "Sam?" He stared at her.

She realized then that with only half her face showing,

recognizing her might be a struggle. She still wore a knit cap, gloves, her coat, and boots. As Sam reached up to pull off her hat, Gracie whimpered.

"She needs to go out. I'm still dressed for the outdoors."

Andy waved his hand. "No way. After what you've been through, I'll take her out. Is there anything special I need to know?"

"No. Just let her choose a good spot for . . . well, you know what."

The whimper became louder.

Andy slipped into his boots. "I don't have a leash for her."

Sam reached into the pocket of the coat she had apparently slept in and pulled out the leash she always kept there. He took it from her and clipped it to Gracie's collar.

Gracie looked up at her as if asking, *Why is the strange man doing this?*

"It's okay, girl. You go out with him."

When Andy opened the door, Gracie sniffed the air and happily went outside.

While they were gone, Samantha checked out his kitchen. She still wasn't one hundred percent sure what had happened last night. She knew she'd been cold. Andy had covered her with warm blankets.

When she pictured him, she sighed. Her teenage self had thought he was very handsome. He'd been the older man she'd dreamed would one day ask her out. Of course, he hadn't because she'd just been Lou's little sister. But if she had to be stranded somewhere . . . Then she remembered what happened when you fell for someone and pushed aside her childish dreams about Andy O'Connell. Steven had ruined that for her for a while, maybe forever.

The dog pulled him along as she sniffed the ground. After she'd done her business, he let her take him to the back of the house. The sun felt good on his face and the dog—Gracie— seemed to be enjoying her outing.

Sam Santoro. He and her brother Lou had been room- mates all four years of college. She'd been the little sister who visited every once in a while. Sam must be about three years younger than them.

When she'd come for her brother's graduation and they'd all gone to dinner, Andy's eyes had stayed on her most of the time. He'd had a hard time looking away from the beautiful woman who had replaced the little girl.

Unfortunately, her brother had noticed. His first words when they stepped into their room that night had been, "Stay away from my little sister."

Andy had tried to argue that she was an adult now, but Lou had followed his earlier words with some that cooled off any romantic feelings he might have held toward Sam. "I love you like a brother, O'Connell, but if you touch my sister, I'm going to have to come after you."

Andy had gulped and nodded. Lou smiled after that, and Andy had never been sure how serious he'd been about the threats, but he also hadn't wanted to test them. In college, Andy had spent his time on the computer while Lou had played football, eventually being considered by the pros. Andy had never forgotten those words by his muscular roommate. He'd stayed close friends with Lou over the years, but he hadn't seen Sam again.

Until today.

Sam pulled off her hat, coat, and boots and ran her fingers through her hair. That would have to do for now. In the kitchen, she pulled a few things from what turned out to be a very well-stocked refrigerator. Gracie needed breakfast and the dog food Sam had brought was in her SUV. In a ditch.

She scrambled up a couple of eggs for her dog and threw in some hamburger and carrots. She scooped that into a bowl from a nearby cupboard and set it on the floor to cool until they returned. She hoped the appeal of food would be greater than Gracie's interest in the four felines who lived here.

Then she thought about the humans in the house and got to work on breakfast for all of them. She scrambled more eggs, adding bacon and cheese to theirs. She'd usually get more creative, but simplicity won today. As she popped bread in the toaster, Andy and Gracie returned.

Gracie happily bounced around Sam.

Andy said, "She was enjoying being outside. I didn't think it would hurt to have her walk around a little bit and get some exercise. I try to do that every day myself." He'd always seemed kind.

"Thank you. I'm sure she loved that. I'm making a quick breakfast for us that will be done soon."

Gracie put her nose in the air and sniffed. She ran over to the cats, who still waited on the sofa. They glared at her as though trying to determine how this invader's presence might play into their lives. A gray-and-white striped one hissed and arched its back in classic Halloween fashion. Gracie wisely took a step back.

"Eat, Gracie."

Her dog turned at those familiar words. Sam crouched in front of the bowl and her dog came running. As Gracie wolfed her food down, Samantha reminded herself that all men, including Andy, were off limits. Maybe especially this man. She'd loved him from afar as a teenager, and it would be all too easy for those emotions to return.

Sam scooped eggs onto two plates and added the toast. "I think I may owe you for my life last night."

Andy had a feeling that that might well have been true. If she'd taken any sort of turn for the worse, he would have had to call for emergency help. Hypothermia could kill very quickly. It seemed harmless, but was far from it.

That still didn't excuse the fact that he had sent her away. "If I hadn't been rude to you in the first place—"

She waved her hand in front of her face to dismiss that. "Let's call it even. My greatest concern right now is getting out of here so I can go back to work."

As soon as she said that, he remembered that she'd come here for Top Tech, and that meant she either needed a website or needed one fixed. "What's your business name?"

A hiss came from behind him. He turned quickly to find that her little black dog had inched closer to the cats.

Sounding like a stern parent, his guest said, "Gracie."

The dog looked back at her with an expression that made Andy laugh. It said, "But Mom?" The dog came over to her owner.

"To answer your question, my business is Goodness Gracie!"

Where had he heard that name before? It was so unusual.

"I make dog treats."

Andy looked up at her. The bad website—no, make that beyond bad. The horrible, unusable, and very terrible website belonged to Sam? "But a gray-haired lady is pictured on it."

"How do you know that?"

"Nathaniel Montgomery called and I looked at it."

She leaned back against the kitchen counter and folded her arms over her chest. "My mother is that woman. And before you ask, no, she isn't a co-owner of the business. The man who made the website for me said he was sure that a mature woman would be more accepted by buyers. He ignored the fact that I had always used a photo of myself. But let's eat and we can talk about this more later." Her voice had a hopeful tone that would be hard to ignore—no matter his workload. She set the plates down on the island and they sat side by side on stools.

When they'd finished what turned out to be light and fluffy eggs, he retrieved his laptop from the coffee table. "I remember from before that your website isn't functional."

"I know." She took the plates over to the sink and rinsed them. "I had a functional website, but *upgraded* to this one. Someone my mother knew builds websites."

Probably someone with time on their hands who thought it would be easy..

"Can you give me the login information to the web host?" Andy kept staring at the computer screen.

"That's the company that keeps the website live, right?"

He looked up at her and grinned. "I've never heard it explained that way, but yes, that does say what a web host is."

"In that case, I do have that information. It's in my purse, which is in my SUV. I left it there because I didn't want to have anything else to carry."

"Then we'd better go get your vehicle." He stood.

Had he said what she thought he had? "Does that mean you're going to help me with my website?"

He held up one hand to stop her. "I still don't have the time, Sam. But I'm going to see if I can at least do something to fix what's here."

"I'll still have mutant animals?"

"It's too early for me to know."

She shrugged. "The good news is that I'm alive and Gracie seems to be undamaged from the experience yesterday." She sat down again.

"Speaking of that, do we need a tow truck, or can the two of us get your vehicle out of wherever it is?"

"I heard a metallic crunching sound as it came to a stop last night. I think it's going to take a tow truck and a whole lot more to get it going again."

He winced when she said that. "That sounds expensive. Do you have good insurance?"

"I did. A friend sold insurance and told me she got me a top-of-the-line plan. A month ago, I downgraded it to save money."

Andy made a call to a towing company he knew. While they waited, Sam went into the bathroom to clean up. She hadn't looked in the mirror earlier and now jumped back when she did. To say she had hat hair would be the understatement of the century.

Andy tapped on the door and she opened it. "There's a

toothbrush and toothpaste kit in that drawer." He pointed to a cabinet. "I keep them in case one of my family members gets stuck here at some point or just decides to hang out longer. If you want to take a shower, you can. There's also a clean robe for guests hooked on the back of the door. We can put your clothes in the wash. Or do you have other clothes in your SUV?"

"I do. I wasn't sure how long I was going to be down here. I always try to be prepared in the winter in case the pass closes and I can't drive home. I even have dog food for Gracie, so we don't have to raid your fridge for her for every meal." When she said those words, she realized she'd committed him to letting her stay longer, but he didn't flinch. It seemed like his mind had already gone there.

"We'll see what the mechanic discovers when it's towed in."

CHAPTER FIVE

*S*am knew she was moving more slowly than normal inside the house, but when she stepped outside and the cold air hit her, she had to hold on to the side of the door frame. Her reaction wasn't from the cold; it was from remembering being out in it last night.

She walked as steadily as she could over to the passenger side of Andy's truck and got in with Gracie jumping in behind her. Andy closed the door behind them, and she leaned back in her seat and relaxed as he drove them back to the scene of her accident.

The tow truck driver had a cable in his hand and was leaning over to attach it to the underside of her SUV.

"I don't even see a scratch from this side," Andy said.

"I hope it was a little scrape on the bottom, like when you drive through a pothole and the edge of it hits something underneath the vehicle but everything is still perfectly fine."

He looked over at her. "That's not what you're expecting, is it?"

"It was a *loud* sound. Maybe that was because everything else was so still and silent."

When the man activated a switch, the SUV slowly rose out of the ditch.

She hopped out and went over to look at where her vehicle had been. A rock stuck up out of the snow.

As soon as the driver had her SUV on level ground again, he walked over and joined them. Pushing his hat back on his head, he looked at the same thing they saw. "Ma'am, that is one big rock you had your vehicle hooked onto."

"Yes. Yes, it is."

"Danny," Andy asked the tow truck driver, who clearly wasn't the stranger she'd presumed, "you know a lot more about cars than I do. Could you—"

"Sure, Andy. Let me check." He set his hat on the hood of his truck, then peered underneath hers. Making a *tsk tsk* sound, he straightened. "Ma'am, I have a strong suspicion this vehicle won't be driving anywhere for a while. You probably need to make some other arrangements. Should I take it to Herb's place?"

She turned to Andy. "Should I?"

He said, "Unless you have somewhere else you'd rather have it go?"

She didn't know anyone in this part of the state other than Andy. To Danny, she said, "If Herb's good, please take it there."

What was she going to do now?

She and Andy transferred everything she'd brought to his truck. As he drove back to his house, Samantha tapped on the elbow rest. She was here with him and had no way to get home. One problem had multiplied into many.

She could fly home, but she wouldn't have her vehicle.

When she'd had her brakes replaced a year ago, she'd learned that the bus didn't run early enough for her to get to the restaurant when she wanted to, and it was much worse on the weekends. And she had to get a full-time job if insurance didn't cover this.

Andy interrupted her thoughts. "I think you're mulling this over just like I am." At her nod, he continued. "We've got several options. One, I can take you to a motel where you can wait out the repair of your SUV."

A combination of anger and sorrow hit her. "I don't have the money to do that, Andy."

"Understandable. You still have a new business."

"No, my business was doing very well. Until I got that website with those crazy animals on it that didn't even work. Almost overnight, I went from making a good income for Gracie and me to not having enough money to pay rent."

He pulled into his driveway and put the truck in park, but left it running with the heat on. "Are you telling me you're broke and homeless?"

"Not yet. And I would never be truly homeless. I have family. And I have enough for two months' rent. But if I can't pay it after that, the clock will be ticking for me to be evicted. I either need to get a functional website—because that's where most of my business is coming from—or I may have to pack everything in my SUV and head south to Idaho to live with Lou. My sisters are out of the country, and my mother downsized to a condo that barely holds her and doesn't allow dogs." She didn't mention going back to work in a restaurant because she wasn't sure if she could handle the daily stress again.

Andy frowned. "Lou has a new baby. right?"

"Yes. A wife, a new baby, *and* two-year-old twins. To say

this isn't ideal is an understatement. I'd have to sleep on the sofa there, but at least I *would* have a place to sleep, and I'd know Gracie and I were safe."

"Okay, then. My option two was to drive you home to Anchorage."

"That could work while they repaired my vehicle. But then I'll have to come back to get it."

"Do you have a roommate you can share rides with until you get your vehicle back?"

She wasn't sure if he was asking if she had a live-in partner she was romantically involved with, or if he meant it in the traditional sense of *roommate*. "Gracie's my only roommate, so I'd be taking the bus. Which might or might not work." She didn't add information he didn't need about the restaurant. "But that still doesn't get me back here later to get my SUV. I'd figure it out when the time came."

Andy rubbed his hand over his face. "Well, then I have a third option to present to you."

She couldn't imagine what that would be. She was a disaster in motion. Her only real choice—other than leaving the state—was to return to Anchorage and go back to Sassy Seafood or work at another restaurant. Every time she thought about restaurant work, though, she could feel her blood pressure rising. For some people, a restaurant kitchen was the best place on earth, but for her, it had been incredibly stressful. "What is it?"

Andy gave Gracie a long stare. She wondered what on earth her dog had to do with his idea.

"If I'd invited you inside yesterday, this accident might not have happened. You can stay with me until your SUV is repaired." As soon as he said the words, he looked like he regretted them.

"In *your* house?" A spark of hope ignited in her. Maybe this *could* all be okay. She could wait here for her SUV to be repaired. Then she thought over everything he'd said. "Andy, I don't want any sort of guilt payback. You don't have to do that because of my accident. I slid off the road. I'm a big girl and I'm responsible for my actions. It isn't your fault or anybody else's. You know, maybe not even mine. I'll sort all of this out on my own. If you take me to the airport in Kenai, I can catch a flight to Anchorage. A friend will pick me up from the airport." She went through her savings in her mind and wondered about the hit on it from her vehicle's repair *and* an airplane ticket.

He tore his gaze from her dog and looked her in the eye. "Sam, I *do* feel responsible for the beat-up SUV that was just towed out of that ditch. You're not only a client who came here to ask for help, but you're also my friend's sister, and look what happened because of me. If you'd left later, that ice patch might have been more frozen and not so slippery. I don't have time to build you an entire website from scratch, but I can promise you that I will get some sort of website up for you."

She clapped her hands with glee. "Thank you! The YouTube videos I'm watching on how to build a website aren't making a whole lot of sense to me."

Andy grinned. "Videos?"

"A girl's gotta do what a girl's gotta do."

His gaze once again went to Gracie. "Until yesterday, my cats had never seen a dog. Well, at least the cats I've had since they were kittens. I just had one adopt me, so I don't know her past."

"Was that the one that let Gracie get close?"

"Yes. Petunia has been living here for a couple of weeks."

"Petunia?" That didn't sound like something a man would name a cat.

He shrugged. "I told my brother Adam about her and his twin daughters came up with the name."

He popped open the door to his truck, started to get out, and turned back toward her. "Let's hold off on major decisions until we get the report back from the mechanic. Maybe it isn't as bad as it seemed and you'll be able to drive out of here soon."

Gracie sat pointed at the door like she was ready to leave. Sam felt in her pocket. There was no leash. Then she remembered Andy had taken Gracie out earlier.

"Andy, I don't want to let Gracie out without a leash on in this unfamiliar place. Would you pick her up and take her in the house or go get the leash for me?"

"I imagine that she'd like to take a little walk around, so I'll get her leash." He jumped out, closed the door and came back a couple of minutes later. He hooked it on the dog and patted his leg. "Come on."

This time, Gracie happily joined him. She must have enjoyed her time outside with him this morning.

Sam reached for Gracie's leash when they arrived at the front door, but Andy stepped back with it in his hand. "You go inside. We'll be inside in a few minutes."

When she opened the door, she found four cats sitting there watching and waiting. It was rather unnerving, like something from a horror movie. They followed her every move as she hung up the coat and went over to the sofa. They didn't approach her, though, choosing to remain at their posts to wait for Andy's return. She hoped they wouldn't be too upset when he returned with the four-legged beast they'd yet to make friends with.

He opened the door, and Gracie blasted into the house.

The cats jumped out of the way, all except the gray cat who sat and watched her. Gracie went over and nuzzled her. Sam had a feeling they could become friends. The other cats' opinions were still up for grabs.

Andy hung the leash on a peg near the door and his coat on a neighboring peg. Then he rather hesitantly said, "Sam, I'm sorry, but I have to get some work done now."

She jumped to her feet. "I'm the one who's sorry! You told me how busy you've been and I took all of this time from your morning."

"No, it's fine. If one of my brothers had stopped by, it would have been the same. But I'm going to go lock myself in my office for the rest of the day. I tend to work late and sleep in. Are you okay on your own?"

"Sure. My laptop spent the night in my vehicle. I didn't expect it to stay there for any amount of time. Do you think it will still work? Or did it freeze into nothingness?"

"I've had a laptop get cold before and it worked fine. But I think I'd let it warm up to room temperature first. Feel free to eat anything you find in the kitchen. I have deli meat and bread to make lunch easy."

Should she offer to cook? She decided to go with his plans today.

Andy turned to go to the opposite side of the house from the bathroom she used earlier. "My office and my bedroom are over here. You can choose any room you want on the other side of the house. Each has its own bathroom."

"But the mechanic may call back today and tell me I can leave."

"He seemed to have other jobs ahead of yours. Let's just

say you're my guest for tonight." He vanished through a doorway.

She turned to her dog. "So how did this happen, Gracie? I dreamed of having a business and that dream turned into a nightmare." She sighed. "What are we going to do today?"

With her computer thawing, she couldn't review her business inventory or other statistics. She checked her phone and didn't find any emails. After flipping through a cooking magazine she'd found on the end table—an odd thing to find in most men's homes—she tossed it to the side. How would she spend her day? She'd love to talk to Kelsey, but this would be a terrible time to call.

Focus on the things you're grateful for. That's supposed to help in times like this. She still had her mother, sisters, brother and his family. She had a warm place to stay with her brother's best friend.

Feeling moderately better—this gratitude thing did seem to work—she leaned back on the sofa and everything started to fold in on her again.

Springing to her feet, she said, "It's time to do something, Gracie. Are you ready to help me in the kitchen? How about trying out a recipe for a new treat?"

At the word *treat*, her dog wagged her tail so hard her whole back end shook.

Sam opened a couple of cupboards and found a large can of salmon, then, no matter what he'd said, felt like she'd crossed a line with his personal space and stopped looking. "What do you think of this, Gracie?" She held it up in the air. Her dog woofed and wagged her tail, but she would do that for almost anything when you asked her a question.

Sam got to work on a treat. She'd been wondering if a dog would love a salmon treat the way a cat would, or at least the way cats in cartoons and comic strips did. When she opened the can of salmon, all the cats wandered over and watched her. She knew dogs should not eat certain things like garlic and onions, but she had no idea what cats' forbidden foods were. She shredded some carrots, steamed them, mixed in some spinach, and added the salmon. Then she put it on a cookie sheet in small dollops and baked it. She missed her trademark squirrel cookie cutter.

Waiting, Sam walked toward the sofa and noticed the opposite side of the room from the wood stove had shelves loaded with books. Instead of succumbing to a designer's wishes and only having a few decoratively placed books on each shelf, they were all filled with titles, but not overfilled. Everything about Andy's home was organized. Maybe it went with the way his mind worked on the websites; each thing had its own compartment.

She browsed through the books, choosing a romance from several. She was surprised to find them in his house—until she noticed that they were all written by Holly O'Connell. Maybe she was the wife of one of his brothers. She knew there had only been boys in the family, and she'd met Jack a time or two. She was glad she'd set the timer because she completely lost track of time in Holly's book.

When she went toward the kitchen, she noticed a fishy scent Andy might not appreciate when he stepped out of his office. Gracie didn't look terribly interested in what she was doing, so this could end up being a complete failure as a trial for dog treats. All treats had to pass the Gracie taste test. The cats, however, were watching her attentively. When she took the pan of treats out and set them on the counter to cool, the gray-and-white striped cat was bold enough to walk over and rub against her leg.

"Do you want one of these?"

A meow was followed by one from one of the other cats. Sam checked her phone and saw that the ingredients were okay for cats, so she went over to Andy's office and knocked on the door.

"I'm sorry to bother you, Andy, but do you mind if I feed your cats carrots and spinach?"

When he opened the door, he had a puzzled expression on his face. "Did you make a salad for my cats?"

She laughed. "No, I made experimental dog treats, but the cats seem more interested in them than Gracie does."

She stood at the entrance to an office that must be every geek's dream. He had an L-shaped desk with three large monitors and a view over the frozen lake.

"Vegetarian dog treats?"

"Salmon."

"Oh! That makes more sense." He shook his head as if to clear it. "You're welcome to give it a try."

She pulled the door closed and turned to find the cats watching her. When she went back toward the island, one of them meowed loudly.

"We have to let these cool before you can eat them, okay?"

She set the tray on the front step for a few minutes to cool. The cats followed her over there, so she carefully closed the door so they couldn't get out. They seemed to know there would be a treat in the offing if they held out. When she opened the door to retrieve the treats a few minutes later, one of the cats rubbed against her leg at the door, startling her.

Movement out of the corner of her eye caught Sam's attention. Looking up, she saw a moose standing not twenty feet from her. She grabbed the treats and pulled them into the house. She didn't think moose ate salmon, but still . . .

She put a treat on a plate and set it down in front of her dog, who hurried over, put her nose to it, backed up three paces, and whimpered.

"Okay, so you don't like salmon. Is that right? Or maybe it's what I put with the salmon." Gracie tentatively stepped forward and gave the treat one more sniff before turning and walking away.

Once the dog was gone, the cats rushed in, but the cat who liked Gracie most sat off to the side and watched.

"Are you less assertive?" She found several small plates and put a treat on each, and then put them out with one right in front of that cat. She gobbled it up and looked at her as if asking was there more? There wasn't anything in it to hurt a cat, so Sam dropped another one on the plate, and the cat at it quickly too.

This cat seemed to like her. At least that was a positive note in a week that hadn't gone well. With Andy working dawn to dusk, she'd be on her own most of the time. They'd have sandwiches for lunch and she'd fix something easy for dinner.

CHAPTER SIX

*a*ndy changed a font on his client's website. Yes, that worked much better. His phone chimed the ring he'd set for his brothers, and Mark's photo filled that screen.

Andy pushed back from his desk. "What's up?"

"I'm just checking in on my little brother. And to thank you again for helping with Maddie's house."

"You're welcome. For the hundredth time."

Mark laughed. "Sometimes she walks around her house touching things like she can't believe it's real."

"Hey, it's your house now too. Are you enjoying married life?" The wistful note in Andy's voice surprised him. He'd had never thought of himself as longing for marriage.

"I highly recommend it. Is anyone on your radar for Mrs. Andy?"

An image of Samantha smiling over breakfast came to mind. Definitely not his type. "I'm too busy working."

"Are you still behind because of the time you spent helping build Maddie's house?"

"I finished those jobs long ago. But I got slammed with

new projects right after the holidays. Actually, it was after your wedding. I guess being involved with you and Maddie leads to my being behind."

Mark chuckled. "I'd like to think that we offer a needed break."

Andy leaned back in his chair. This had been a season of weddings. First, Mark and Maddie's the week before Christmas, and then Noah and Rachel's on Valentine's Day. Both couples had been beyond happy before and after the ceremonies.

"Maddie and I had dinner with Nathaniel and Jemma the other night. He has some suggestions for marketing my contracting services."

Andy sat upright. "Are you having trouble getting work?"

"There's no need to worry. I can find jobs, but I'd like to do the higher end stuff. I'm finding more and more that I enjoy the special details and carpentry. The average homeowner doesn't have a budget that allows for much of that."

"But I bet you've added special touches anyway."

"Well, I want to make sure every house is a dream house. Nathaniel also mentioned that he had a client he'd told you about, one who makes pet treats and desperately needed a website. But you turned down the referral."

That seemed like an odd topic of conversation for the two of them. "I didn't have time. He must be very interested in this client's business."

Mark laughed, but it sounded . . . off. A bit forced. "From what I can tell, he's interested in all of his clients' businesses."

Andy knew that was true. Maybe nothing was wrong.

"Anyway, Nathaniel said the client couldn't find another web designer."

He had to be talking about Sam. "There are many, many talented web designers."

"Yeah, well, Nathaniel suggested to her that you would be the most affordable."

Andy swiveled his chair to the right, the direction of what he'd already come to think of as Sam's wing of his house. "That's why he chose me? Because I'm cheap?"

"Of course not. You're talented *and* cheap." This time his laugh sounded more normal.

Andy grinned. "I appreciate the compliment. I think."

Mark paused and hesitated. "Are you sure you don't have time?"

Andy had never had a brother interested in his client list before. "I'm sure."

Mark sighed. "Okay, then. Will we see you Saturday at Mom and Dad's?"

"Mom threatened to move lunch to my house if I didn't call and confirm by Friday night."

Mark chuckled. "I know you don't have time to cook for a crowd, so I guess your answer is that I *will* see you."

Andy thought of Gracie. Would she and her pet parent still be at his house on Saturday? Probably. Gracie might enjoy meeting fellow canines Emma and Zeke. But what would the rest of his family, especially his mother, have to say about Sam being here? Learning that an available single woman was living here—and one his mother had met— might send her matchmaking radar into overdrive. "I'll confirm on schedule and meet you at *their* house."

"Great! I know Noah and Rachel are coming this week."

They said their goodbyes. Andy set his phone down on the desk beside him.

Both Nathaniel and Mark wanted him to work with Samantha. Were they matchmaking?

He chuckled. He was seeing matchmakers everywhere. Mark had never met Sam, and Nathaniel was looking out for a client.

He pulled a snack out of his desk drawer and turned back to his computer. Just a few more hours of work and he could go to bed.

CHAPTER SEVEN

*S*am set her book on the nightstand and turned out the light. She smiled as an image of Andy O'Connell popped into her head, but not this Andy. She saw the man she'd met during her brother's freshman year of college. Andy had been handsome, smart, and kind to her—everything a teenage girl would want in a man. He'd also been younger then and less confident.

She'd gone home and written about him in her diary, one she kept safely locked and in a box in her closet lest her mother discover she pined after someone three years older than her.

Her family had invited Andy for Thanksgiving one year because he hadn't wanted to fly home for the short break and their home in Idaho wasn't too far from the Oregon university. Her high school boyfriend had been there too, but Andy had outshined him in every way.

Lou's graduation had been a family-filled event and the last time she'd seen Andy—until yesterday. If anything, he had grown more handsome.

These thoughts got her nowhere. A man was the last thing she needed in her life right now, especially one who lived hours away from her and seemed completely uninterested in anything other than work. Sighing, she turned out the light.

No daylight filtered through the curtains when she next opened her eyes. The unfamiliar clock on the nightstand said 6:00 a.m. Then she remembered where she was and what had brought her here. Repairs to her vehicle could easily eat up much of the money she had left.

Years working in the restaurant industry had taught her to get up early, and she'd had a hard time breaking that habit since she'd quit working there. She'd overslept, so maybe she was making progress. Or maybe she'd simply been exhausted from her ordeal.

Sam opened doors in the hallway, hoping to find a laundry room on her side of the house so she wouldn't wake Andy up by washing her clothes. She grinned when the second door opened to a room that had everything she needed. She threw all of her clothes into the washer and headed back to bed to read while she waited. When she put them in the dryer, she took a shower. Then, dressed in her still-warm clothes, she took Gracie out for her morning walk. When they returned, her dog curled up on the floor next to the couch, probably to keep an eye out for the cats who frequently sat on it.

Wanting to be quiet, Sam retrieved Holly's book from her bedroom and sat on the couch to continue reading it. The attraction between the couple was obvious to the reader, but not yet to the characters. A while later, she looked up from her book and her black dog had disappeared. She hoped she hadn't gotten into any mischief. After searching most of the living area, she found Gracie snuggled up next to the gray kitty beside one of the chairs. They made a pretty picture.

When Gracie lifted her head to look at her, Sam said, "It's okay. You can stay with your new friend." Gracie put her head back down and closed her eyes.

At some point, this kitty may have been near a dog. Or maybe she'd been on her own so long she would accept all friends. Sam glanced over toward Andy's door, wishing that humans could all be that way.

She grabbed her phone and went back to her bedroom so she could call Kelsey without waking Andy.

"Are you coming in today?"

Her friend's excitement made her grin for a moment, and then she remembered her situation.

"Change of plans. I slid off the road and my SUV's in the shop."

"Call a taxi."

"In Kenai."

"Whoa. Give me the whole story."

Sam gave her the condensed version since she knew her friend had to go back to work. "And that's it."

Kelsey laughed. That wasn't the reaction Sam had expected.

"You have an accident and end up staying with the handsome friend of your brothers who you crushed on when you were younger. Did I get that right?"

"You did."

"Only you, Sam." A shout came through the line, and Kelsey whispered, "Pieter's yelling about prep not being done. I have to get back to work."

Sam stared at her phone. There went the perfect example of working in a restaurant. She went back to the great room and sat in the chair next to the pets with her laptop on her lap. "Let's hope it works, Gracie." When the computer started, she said, "Yes!" and did a fist pump. Her dog sleepily wagged her tail.

After checking her email and finding no new orders from previous customers, Sam closed the lid in frustration and put the computer on the coffee table. They must take one look at the website and run. Unlike her, Andy had work to do. She was an intrusion in his normal life, but she'd like to at least be a helpful intrusion.

Andy said he worked late, so maybe she could make a breakfast that he could eat whenever he got up, but that she could eat now. She opened the refrigerator and found inspiration. Eggs, vegetables, bacon, and ham called out to be made into a frittata, Italy's open-faced, baked version of an omelet. It could not only be heated up for Andy when he was ready but also be eaten as leftovers tomorrow.

She hoped Andy would like what she'd made. Then again, she'd gathered everything out of the man's refrigerator, so he should. As she slid the pan in the oven, she felt a cat bump against her leg and heard one of Gracie's soft *woofs*. Both animals sat and stared at her. Sam put Gracie's food in her bowl and she dove in, but the kitty continued looking up at her. Other than salmon treats, what did cats eat?

"I'm sorry, but I don't know how to help you."

The cat continued watching her as she cleaned up her cooking mess.

Andy came out from a different door than his office's, wearing faded jeans, a T-shirt that said "Geeks are the Real Rock Stars," and a bleary-eyed expression. She knew he'd worked late when he said, "The cats woke me up." He yawned before continuing. "They let me know it was time for their breakfast in no uncertain terms, but I leave food for them overnight they can snack on. So they *don't* have to wake me up."

Sam chewed on her lip. "The cats' bowls are on the floor, and one of your guests is basically a garbage disposal on four legs."

He rubbed his eyes and looked over to where she'd gestured at Gracie, who was finishing up her breakfast.

"That never occurred to me."

At least he didn't sound angry.

"Life with a dog?" She added a happy lilt to the end of the sentence, hoping the happiness would reach him.

Gracie stopped eating, sat, and cocked her head sideways, what Sam considered one of her most adorable poses.

He chuckled. "She's a cute dog."

Score one for Gracie.

Andy went over to a cupboard Sam hadn't opened and pulled out some cans of food. Then he looked from Gracie to his cats. "I think we may have to move the food up to the far end of the kitchen counter while Gracie's here. Let's not do any food prep over there."

"I agree that's probably the best thing."

Andy kneeled in front of the cat. "Petunia isn't able to jump that high anymore. Until she has her kittens, she'll need a separate place to eat."

"Kittens?" That explained the cat's appetite and girth.

"Petunia is expecting any day. She was on my doorstep a month or so ago when I opened my door. I'm a long way from any other occupied house this time of year. She had to have been quite lost. Once I'd fed her, she happily came inside and made herself at home. I don't know how she survived the winter, but she must have been curled up in wood piles and hunting mice."

Did this man's kindness never end? At least she understood now why he had taken in her and Gracie when he didn't have to. He could have easily driven her to the airport and left it at that. Her brother would have thought he'd done enough.

She grinned broadly. "Maybe the kittens will come while we're here."

"The way this week has gone, they probably will."

She wasn't sure if he meant that in a positive way. She suspected not.

As he went out to the garage, presumably to find something he could use to make a safe place for his fourth kitty to eat, he stopped in the kitchen and sniffed. "Please don't tell me that delicious scent is coming from whatever you fed that dog."

"Gracie." She corrected without even thinking about it. "No. That's our breakfast frittata."

Then he cocked his head to the side. "You do know how to cook, right? I mean, other than dog treats."

As soon as Andy said the words, he regretted them. What if she didn't know how to cook at all? What if she was in line to be a contestant on that cooking show featuring terrible cooks? He tried for a casual tone and leaned against the counter in what he hoped was an equally casual position. "Do you cook often at home?"

Samantha grinned. "Worried about the tastiness of breakfast, are you?"

He shrugged sheepishly, then held up his thumb and fore-finger an inch apart. "Maybe a bit."

Sam laughed. "Andy, I'm a chef."

That expression was thrown around so often he wasn't even sure what she meant. "As in you cooked professionally somewhere or you're just a good cook?"

Sam picked up her phone from the island, scrolled through pages on it, and handed it to him.

The article on the screen was titled, "L.A. hotshot chef joins Anchorage's restaurant scene." A photo of Sam in chef's whites filled the screen. He read the beginning of the story. "You're the executive chef in one of the best restaurants in Anchorage?"

"I was until I left to run Goodness Gracie!"

He put his hand on his chest. "Be still, my heart. I may have been woken up by the cats so they could eat, but at least I'll have something delicious for myself." He continued toward the garage. "Let me get Petunia set up. I'm now looking forward to breakfast."

He used wood scraps from other projects to make what looked like a baby gate to keep the other cats and the dog out of the area at the end of the kitchen. When he'd finished that, he sat on a stool at the island, hoping Sam's cooking skills lived up to his expectations.

The last woman who had cooked for him had left quite an impression. He'd had to go to the ER for emergency care and had never gone out with her again—not because he wouldn't date someone who couldn't cook, but because she kept screaming in the ER that she was sorry and why did this keep happening on dates? They'd had to escort her out. It had been a horrible scene.

He took a bite of what turned out to be eggs lightly

flavored with herbs. She'd used the cheese he'd bought on his last trip to Anchorage, the imported French brie. And sun-dried tomatoes. He set down his fork and closed his eyes.

"Andy, are you okay? Is there something wrong with your food?"

He opened his eyes and saw her staring at him with concern.

"It's wonderful. The best frittata I have ever eaten." He took a bite of the biscuit she'd served with butter and some blueberry jam he'd made last fall. It melted in his mouth. After he swallowed it, he said, "You are an amazing chef. I seem to remember Lou being upset that you didn't want to go to college."

"I worked in restaurants in high school and knew I wanted to be a chef, so I went to culinary school in Paris for a year. Then I worked my way up the ladder."

He savored another bite. "I was good on computers when I was young. Did you always want to cook?"

"When I was about ten, I wanted to be a painter."

"Well, you are certainly an artist with this food."

She laughed. "That's a good thing because it turned out that I was a terrible painter."

Andy laughed and started choking. After a few gulps of water, he said, "Then it looks like you went the right direction. Is that why you make dog treats now? Is it something you did on the side while you worked as a chef?"

She set her fork down. "Andy, you have no idea of the stress in a restaurant kitchen. I was there long hours, seven days a week. I had to come in hours before we opened to do the prep work and stay until we closed so I could help clean the kitchen." She cringed. "I worked as a sous chef in California and then moved to Alaska about a year ago. I was thrilled to step into an executive chef position at one of the top restaurants in Alaska's largest city. I was used to fourteen- to sixteen-hour days, but I couldn't take the pressure of running the show. I started unwinding by making dog treats for the puppy I wanted but didn't have time to take care of. When I brought some in to the restaurant and gave them to a coworker, her dog loved them so much that everybody who owned a dog ordered some."

Andy took another bite of his frittata. "So, you quit?"

"I went to the farmer's market to buy produce for the restaurant one morning and drove by the animal shelter. I'd been *unwinding* so much that I had a surplus of treats, so I stopped to see if they'd like some. Then one of the best things to ever happen took place. When I went inside, I found the front desk person on the phone. She put her hand over the phone and said, 'Go ahead and look around,' then motioned me to the left. So I did."

"And you found Gracie?"

She looked over at her dog, who had inched forward toward the cats. There seemed to be a standoff. "It was love at first sight. I went to the restaurant with the produce I'd bought and gave my notice."

"You named your business for her."

"She loved the treats so much that she gobbled them up. I said, 'Goodness Gracie!'" Sam finished her breakfast and took her plate to the sink, returning for his. "Would you mind if I made lunch for us? It will give me something to do."

He grinned. "Are you kidding? You can spend all the time in the kitchen that you want to as long as I get to eat the results."

"Should I set aside dog treats for you to try too?" She raised an eyebrow.

Andy chuckled. "I'll let the superior canine and feline taste buds sample those."

"If you're sure. Are there any things you don't like?" She held up one hand. "Wait. If you didn't like something, you wouldn't have it in the house."

"There is one thing that I keep here because of my dad: potato chips with vinegar on them." He shuddered.

"I like those." She grinned at what he knew was a look of horror on his face. "You're probably safe, though, because I doubt I'd be able to incorporate them into a meal."

"That's a relief! Then anything you find is fair game. There's a big freezer in the garage, with pretty much any meat you might want, including some fish I caught last summer and berries I picked with my family last fall."

"I'll browse and see what I find."

"And I'm sorry, but I may be a little late to lunch," he continued. "I'm finishing a website and getting it to my client this morning. They *always* ask for significant changes when I think I'm done. The best I can hope for is work I can finish in a day. I've had them ask me to completely redo the site I'd just finished, changes that took almost a week." He was frowning when he stopped speaking.

"And that makes you less than happy?"

She had a way of making him smile. "Yes, it does. But I'll do my best to stay focused on the wonderful meal you'll make."

He went into his office and closed the door behind him. Sam had brought sparkle into his isolated winter world. She intrigued him, but he didn't want to find any woman intriguing. Lori had charmed him initially and look where that had gotten him. He didn't want to love and lose someone again. Ever.

As he worked, the scene out his window kept dragging him away from his computer screen. Sunshine shimmered off snow crystals, making the outdoors a winter wonderland. In a month, maybe less, much of the snow would be gone. His guest must be getting bored, and he wished he could be outside. If only he had time, he could fix both of those problems at once.

Lucy and Kitty jumped onto his file cabinet and watched the scene out the window too. "Have you escaped the dog, girls?" Cat doors on his office and bedroom doors allowed them to visit him whenever they wanted.

Andy forced his attention back to the job at hand. A short time later, he sent a link to the new version of the site to his client for approval. He'd give them a half hour to send it back with changes. At least they usually responded quickly. Before he got involved in a different project, he wanted to finish this one.

Leaning back in his chair, he stared out the window. Happy chose that moment to jump onto his lap.

"You're an opportunist, aren't you?"

The black-and-white tuxedo cat put her paw on his chest and licked him on the chin, then curled up.

"You knew I needed to get away from the computer for a few minutes." He petted her as he watched the view change with the light.

His computer pinged, letting him know he'd received an email. Andy lifted Happy to the floor and rolled back to his desk.

The client wrote: *It's great. Thank you. We'll have a new project in a few weeks.*

Andy read the words three times. No changes? He jumped to his feet and ran out the door. "Sam!"

She leaped off the couch. "What's wrong?"

"That client accepted the site as is! I have other jobs, but nothing else promised for today. I thought I'd be busy." He hugged her, and a zing went through him. He stepped back and stared at her. She was his guest, and that was inappropriate. But he wished he could hold her again.

She blushed, but didn't make any comment. "What's your plan?"

"I've longed to be outside today. It's beautiful and the temperatures are around freezing. Would you like a snowmobile ride?"

A smile lit her face. Every time she did that, it reached inside him and healed him a bit more. "I'd love that." Then she looked at her dog. "But I don't know if I can leave Gracie alone with the cats. Except this one, of course." She motioned him over and he found her dog and Petunia curled up together.

Laughing, he said, "The other three have been with me this morning. They have cat doors, so they can escape the strange animal that's visiting their domain."

"Then I would love to get outside." She hurried toward the door and grabbed her coat off the hook. "I'm not used to sitting still. There's only so much I want to do in your pretty kitchen."

As they got their outdoor gear on, he said, "Think of it as your home while you're here. Mess it up all you want."

Sam laughed. "You may regret those words."

"I doubt that. Get your gloves and follow me."

She shoved her gloves in her pockets, and he led her to the door that went to stairs and the basement. Once downstairs, he said, "I'll start the snowmobile and move it outside." As he walked toward the side room that stored that and his other outdoor equipment, he asked, "Where have you been on snowmobiles?"

"Nowhere."

He stopped and turned toward her. "My first thought was, why? Then I realized I've lived out here long enough that I assume everyone has the same access to the outdoors. You live in the big city."

"It's more than that. I didn't have time. But I'm looking forward to this!"

He chuckled. "I hope it lives up to your expectations." He opened the door to the storage area. "I have two machines, one for a single person and one for two because Mom loves going out but refuses to drive one herself. We take turns with her." When he went in, he told her, "I'll move the snowmobile outside and close the door, then you can hop on behind me."

A few minutes later, Sam climbed onto the snowmobile behind him.

Over the engine, he said, "Hold on to me. We'll go over some rough terrain and uphill."

He would think of Sam as a little sister. He'd tell Lou that he'd taken his sister out for fun when she'd been stuck here.

As soon as she put her arms around him, he knew he had miscalculated. Instead of a simple zing, this time her warmth made him feel cared for.

Distractions could get them killed. Pushing those thoughts away, he gave the machine gas, and they took off. He shouted, "It's late enough in the winter that I'm staying away from lakes and rivers that might not be frozen solid anymore." He didn't add his next thought because it might scare her on her first time out. *And away from mountains since avalanches are possible.*

Samantha wrapped her arms around Andy's waist and held on as the snowmobile surged forward and around his house. Nature zoomed by as he drove deeper and deeper into the backcountry. A pine-tree lined path covered with snowmobile tracks took them higher. They went up a hill, down the other side, then over and around what must be a small frozen stream. Minutes later, Andy pointed to their left, and she saw a moose in the distance. He finally came to a stop on the top of another hill. A mountain range glistened in the distance, and the sun warmed her face.

"Look at the view, Sam."

She'd been so focused on what was right around her that she hadn't noticed the stunning view. White snow with green trees went far into the distance. "That is spectacular." She fished her phone out of her pocket and snapped photos.

"Settle back in for the ride home. I want to get there long before dark."

She tucked her phone into her pocket. Being stuck in the cold again was the last thing she wanted right now, so she got back into position and they took off. When they arrived at his house, Andy pulled up to the front door and handed her his keys. "You can go inside, and I'll put this away."

"That was amazing, Andy! Thank you." She wanted to hug him again, but he'd seemed put off by the concept earlier. She put the key in the lock and went inside. Gracie bounded over to her, so she hooked on her leash and took her outside.

When Andy had taken care of the snowmobile, he went up the stairs. Delicious scents wafted past him as he pulled open the basement door. His personal chef had made lunch. He found her at the stove. "I smell something wonderful."

"I made us some Monte Cristo sandwiches and a salad on the side. Does that work for you? It was fast and easy."

He sniffed the air. "I know it's going to taste as good as it smells—"

"Or better." She grinned.

Andy chuckled. "Or better. I'm fine with that. You didn't incorporate any of those vinegar chips, did you?"

"Not a chance. But I don't like the sandwiches dusted with powdered sugar as some people do, so I haven't done that. If you want it, I can add it."

"No. That's okay."

Lunch rivaled breakfast. Sam had a gift for making simple food special.

Andy wondered if he should call Lou and tell him his sister was his houseguest. Would he be upset that they were alone together? He might be. They talked about once a month, so he'd tell him *if* he called while she was his guest. He decided to avoid that conversation as long as he could.

"Sam, I can take a few minutes to look at your site when we're done."

"Thank you!" She grinned from ear to ear. "For that, I'll make a special dinner."

CHAPTER EIGHT

*A*ndy scrolled through the page on his computer screen, trying to figure out what had happened to Sam's site. He'd tried the usual fixes for a nonfunctioning website, but it remained frozen. The animals were the only things that moved.

She sat patiently across from him, reading one of the books he'd had on his shelf for quite a while. He never had brought himself to actually read one of Holly's books. Romance novels weren't his thing, but he guessed that a lot of men felt the same way. His brother Adam had once said that he'd been surprised, though, because he actually liked his wife's books.

Sam smiled at something she read, and it lit up her face, making her even prettier.

Don't go there, O'Connell. The phone lying on the couch cushion beside him rang with the music he'd set for his brothers, and Noah's picture appeared on the screen.

He answered. "Taken any interesting flights lately?"

"They don't get any more interesting than the one where

I met Rachel, so I guess I'd have to say no. A flight today had some tense moments, though. A passenger had a heart attack between Homer and Anchorage."

"Is he okay?"

"We've been told that *she's* going to be fine. The ambulance was waiting on the runway in Anchorage; we pulled up to it, and they rushed her to the hospital."

"That's certainly more interesting than my work."

"Could that be because you're sitting there alone and surrounded by snow? You need to get out more. Maybe meet a lovely lady."

Andy's gaze lifted toward Sam. She certainly fit the *lovely* requirement. She seemed to know he was watching her because she looked up from her book and smiled.

"We're fine here."

Noah laughed. "You and your furry ladies."

"Hey, they're good company."

"Are you keeping busy with work?"

Andy stared at the screen in front of him, the job he didn't really have time to do on top of all the others. "More than busy. I think things are going to get better soon, though. I'm almost caught up."

A moment of silence greeted him. Every time that happened with one of his brothers, he wondered what was up. He felt like a parent noticing that the kids were suddenly quiet and wondering what they were up to. With five boys, his mother had probably come running when that had happened.

"I know of a job for you. Nathaniel was helping Rachel with her marketing and mentioned a client who needs a website."

"Is that so?" Andy put his hand over his racing heart. *Not matchmaking with Sam. Please not that!*

Noah continued speaking. "Yes, this person apparently has a website that a family friend worked on, and it doesn't work at all anymore."

Andy made a strangled sound, and Sam looked at him.

She asked in a low voice, "Everything okay?"

He gave a single nod, then shook his head from side to side. This was a bigger mess than he'd realized. "You don't say. Well, I'm so busy right now that I don't think I can take on any new jobs. Do you have any more information about this client?"

He knew none of his brothers would lie to him, but he wondered how much Noah would actually say.

"I don't know too much about the business—" Andy noticed that his brother never said whether it was a male or female potential client "—but it has something to do with pet food. I know that doesn't sound appealing, but Nathaniel said it was an interesting project and that you would probably get a lot out of it."

Like a wife. It was time to change the subject. "Are you coming to Mom and Dad's tomorrow?"

"Both Rachel and I are coming this time. Between the Christmas season and our wedding, she missed a lot of the lunches."

Andy forced a happy tone into his voice. "I'll see you then."

When they signed off, Andy jumped to his feet and dropped the phone onto the couch. Then he whirled around and faced Sam.

"We've been set up!" He said every word deliberately and with emphasis.

She stared at him like he had lost his mind.

"What are you talking about? Nathaniel told me about you and your website-building abilities just like he told me about a printer when I needed a brochure."

Andy stared at the offending phone. "I didn't tell you this, but my brother Mark called earlier in the week. I guess it was two days ago."

She shrugged. "And?"

"And he tried to get me to work for you. He told me all about this client who needed a new website—" he held up his hand when she started to speak "—and not just any website, but one that had gotten messed up and had something to do with pet treats."

She grinned. "What did you tell him?"

"I told him the same thing I told you. That I was too busy to work on your website."

Sam's happy expression changed to sadness when she heard those words. "So, a second brother called, or was it someone else in your family?"

"No, this was my brother Noah."

Sam raised her hands in a shrug. "I don't see the problem. They're playing matchmaker. You don't want to be matched. End of story. Isn't it?"

Andy looked at her and nodded slowly. "You're right. They're trying to fix us up, but that doesn't mean we have to accept it. Does it?"

Sam watched the handsome man in front of her, a man who normally smiled, took care of his cats in a loving way, and was smart and a hard worker. She couldn't ask for much more, at least not for someone she'd be willing to go out on a date or two with. But he seemed to be against all relationships. "Tell me, Andy, why is it that matchmakers upset you so much?"

He looked at her with disbelief. "Are you kidding? I don't want anybody messing with my life."

That made sense to her. Maybe in time he would be interested in something more with her. Not that she was interested in that with him. She'd had enough of trying to drag a reluctant groom to the altar.

"Besides, I'm not sure that I ever want to get married." he said. "I'm happy. If you're happy, why do you need to change anything?"

"You have a good point."

He smiled at that moment, maybe because he thought he was off the hook with her.

"Then again . . ."

The scowl returned.

"Sometimes change can be a good thing." With that, she stood. "Let's figure out what to make for dinner tonight. Something different, perhaps?" She grinned at him.

Just as she'd expected and hoped, Andy grinned back. He bounced back pretty quickly. In the kitchen, Samantha sorted through the produce in Andy's vegetable drawer. "How often do you go to the store?"

"About once a week. What have we got in there?"

Samantha paused at the use of the word "we." She ruthlessly pushed down the part of her heart that did a little happy dance at that moment. She had too much going on to want a man in her life, especially one who didn't live anywhere near her. He definitely wasn't the one for her.

Besides, she didn't want any man right now. The last one had broken her heart.

"Carrots, onions, cabbage, and broccoli. All the winter keeper kind of things." She rustled around in the meat drawer. "The meat we got out yesterday is still pretty hard. But I think I could slice off some of it." She turned toward him. "It is so nice being in a house with sharp knives. You actually know how to cook."

Andy laughed. "I've done my best to learn how. Living alone and enjoying good food helped push me into it."

Sam reached behind her and waved a hand. "My sisters all live alone, and not one of them knows how to cook."

"Why didn't you learn together when you were kids?"

"They're all older than I am and weren't interested. All three of them are smart and earn a great income, but they would come close to starvation or malnutrition if it weren't for restaurants and premade food."

Andy chuckled.

"What about you with a whole mess of brothers? Do you and your brothers make awesome meals together?"

Andy laughed. "They don't cook for me. Not if I want to enjoy the meal. My brother Jack is a terrible cook. For some reason, I'm the only one of the five of us who is interested in cooking. I've found that interest is what you need to do something well."

His reasoning was sound. Sam grabbed the meat out of the fridge and put it on the cutting board on the island. Then she got to work slicing it very thinly for stir-fry. Andy gathered some ingredients from his cupboard and the fridge and put them next to the cutting board. When she glanced over and found soy sauce, fish sauce, mirin, and toasted sesame oil, she grinned. Her fiancé Steven hadn't been able to fry an egg. That didn't really bother her in a potential spouse, but it was nice to be here with someone who shared that interest.

Andy said, "I got some rice going in the rice cooker. I assume you want minced garlic."

Sam laughed. "Do fish swim?"

Andy chuckled. "I'm also a garlic fan, so our time here together should be flavorful."

Without thinking, she said, "And two garlics cancel each other out."

He stopped and stared at her.

As she felt her face turning hot, she looked up at him. "What I meant to say was that when two people eat garlic, the air can become very garlicky." The reference had been about kissing someone who'd eaten garlic, and Andy seemed to have picked up on that. But she didn't want to go there.

Before long, they had prepared a stir-fried meal that included shredded carrots, cabbage, garlic, broccoli, and beef. They served it over the steamed rice.

Sam tasted the food and nodded her approval. "We came up with a great dinner, but you'll probably need to run to the store in the next day or two."

Andy nodded and closed his eyes as he took a bite. "This is delicious. I need to remember this for the future."

"The recipe?"

He grinned. "No. To make sure that all the beautiful women who drive into the ditch near me are trained chefs."

Sam stared at him. He thought she was beautiful. That was the first personal comment he'd made about her. His face turned bright red, and he shoved another bite of food in his mouth. But it didn't matter. He couldn't take back *beautiful*.

To give him a break, she changed the subject. "Your house seems fairly new. When did you build it?"

"I finished it about a year ago. I spent a few months planning it and then about six months in construction. My brothers and dad helped when they could."

"Why all the way out here? Not that it isn't gorgeous," she added when he looked up at her.

"I think I wanted to escape people. Not completely, though. You *can* do that in Alaska. I wanted to get away from cities and towns."

She couldn't see anything except the dark night beyond the windows but remembered from her lonely hike after her accident that he had certainly achieved isolation. "Was there a reason?"

Andy looked up at her as though he'd forgotten what they were talking about.

"A reason you wanted to get away from people?"

His face became shuttered. "Yeah." Then he stood without giving any more information and said, "I always feel like I should have an orange or something like that for dessert when I eat Asian foods, not cake or cookies."

His one-word answer didn't satisfy her. She debated for about three seconds about asking for more about his reasons, then decided he looked too upset. It must have been a woman. She shifted her mind to dessert. "I like oranges. If that's what you've got, bring it on."

He raised one finger in the air. "On second thought, I have some orange sorbet in the freezer."

"That would be the best of both worlds, wouldn't it?" She smiled at him in what she hoped was an encouraging way.

The phone rang as he scooped the sorbet into a bowl—with an ice cream scoop, of course. Andy had the correct implement for everything. She grabbed his phone off the couch and took it over to him.

His scowl deepened when he looked at it.

"Not a friend?"

"Mom. I love her dearly, but I'm not expecting this call, and that usually means something isn't right."

He answered the phone. "Mom! How are you?"

He set the phone on the counter as he worked, assuming there was nothing private in the conversation. She'd called with video, so he made sure to face it away from Sam.

"I'm fine, son. You've apparently had a very busy week."

He had at that. He glanced over at Samantha as she took a bite of sorbet from the bowl he'd slid over to her. He glanced at his mom's photo on the screen at that moment and noticed the day of the week on the screen. *Friday.*

As he was about to say that he was sorry for not calling earlier and that he *would* be at lunch tomorrow, his mother continued. "I've already called everyone to let them know we're having lunch at your house tomorrow." Her smile was a little too gleeful. "Holly can't come because she's doing something with her sisters, so she won't be bringing pies for dessert."

He stared at his phone. *Please say you're kidding.*

"From your dumbstruck expression, my guess is you haven't started making the meal yet."

Andy shook his head slowly from side to side.

"Then you may want to consider the menu. I have no doubt that everything you make will be delicious. I shudder to think of imposing on Jack." *As would they all.*

Then she gave a tired sigh. "It's lovely having one of my boys take over on a Saturday so I can relax and read. Tomorrow, I'll just be a guest and not be concerned about all the details of the day." She fanned herself with her hand, as though thinking about it exhausted her.

Andy's gaze narrowed. He knew his mother adored every second of the days they came to her house, but she was working him, trying to appeal to his compassionate side. Everyone knew he had one.

Sam raised an eyebrow when he looked over at her.

"I haven't thought about tomorrow yet."

"We'll see you about eleven. And it looks like all of your brothers, except Adam, are bringing their significant others —because they each have one—so that makes nine guests for lunch." She gave a little finger wave and said, "Toodle-oo. See you then."

Sam was clearly trying to hold her laughter, but a rough snort escaped.

His mother asked, "What was that odd noise? Are your cats okay?"

He wanted to glare at Sam, but he didn't dare look that direction and prove that someone else was here. Lucy jumped onto the counter, a place she knew she was not allowed to go, but her timing couldn't have been better. She stepped in front of the phone and sat down. Sometimes he loved having his cats more than other times, and this was one of the best ones.

"Is that Lucy?"

"It is."

"I'm looking forward to seeing her and the other cats tomorrow. Bye." And the screen went blank.

73

Sam burst into laughter. "She's cute. What are you cooking?"

Andy slowly looked at Sam. "I don't think you've put the pieces together on this."

Her brow furrowed, and then, all of a sudden, her eyes widened, and she jumped to her feet. "I'm here and they don't know I'm here. Is there going to be a shotgun wedding?"

Andy rolled his eyes. "Of course not. I know that when Rachel and Noah were alone together, everyone believed them that everything was fine. Besides, you have your own wing of the house. It's just you and the cats at night."

"Well, me and Petunia. She's the only one who isn't afraid of Gracie. But at least the others are warming up to her. What are we going to do? Can you take me to a friend's house?"

"I don't think so. My parents know all of my friends, and I think the whole story would filter back to them. There's a room in the basement that I only use in the summer. It opens to the backyard, so it's very convenient to come and go without trudging through the rest of the house. Maybe you and Gracie could go down there for the day." At that moment, Gracie started barking at some perceived infraction outside the window.

"Gracie!" The dog stopped and turned to look at Sam with a "What, Mom?" expression.

Andy said, "There will be two other dogs outside. Maybe people will think that's where the barking is coming from."

Sam sat back down and started laughing. Tears squeezed out of her eyes, and she wiped them off her cheeks. "Do you really think that two dogs are not going to bark at another dog, and that dog is not going to answer? The combined noise would be so loud that the neighbors would wonder what was going on—if you had neighbors this time of year."

She was right. His options dwindled to zero. "I guess there's only one thing that we can do. You'll have to be here for lunch."

CHAPTER NINE

*A*ndy smiled often, but not now. He picked up Lucy in his arms and stalked across his living room to stare at the window, which now only reflected back the lights inside the house. Then he turned and walked back to Sam, stared at her, spun on his heels, and did another lap. The cat pushed herself out of his arms and jumped down, looking up at him indignantly.

"We have a huge problem here."

His tension made her nervous. "I thought we decided that there wouldn't be a shotgun wedding or any repercussions for my being here."

Andy stared at her. "No repercussions? I never said or implied that. My family is a herd of matchmakers. A *giant* herd of matchmakers. For years, it was only my mother. We fought off her matchmaking attempts all our lives. Well, maybe not when we were little kids." He waved his hand in front of himself. "You know what I mean."

Sam laughed. "I do. But I still don't understand the problem."

"You haven't met my mother. Ha! She's known for making phenomenally bad choices for each of us. All five of us have stories of her attempts. Last fall, she sent someone to me who 'needed fishing lessons.'" He put air quotes around the last part of the sentence. "She'd lived in Alaska for a year or two and never learned to fish. I knew what Mom was doing. I think the woman, Shelley, did too. Well, Shelley hated every aspect of fishing. The day was bad from start to finish. When the boat docked at the end of it, Shelley admitted she didn't even like to eat fish!"

Sam laughed. "Your mother sounds like a strong woman. She clearly loves you, or she wouldn't fix you up over and over again."

He stopped what he was doing and focused on her. "She wants grandchildren. Babies. Adam married Holly when her girls were already in school. Mom's fantasy includes her sons bringing their babies to her house every Saturday. Of course, she loves us. But . . ."

He went over to where he'd left his computer on the kitchen island and started fiddling around with something on it—to have something else to focus on, Sam assumed. That sounded like a good plan.

"First, Adam and Holly got together. We had a gap for a year or so, and everything quieted down. The remaining four of us talked about feeling a sense of relief. Then Noah found Rachel. Due to a matchmaker. And Mark got a second chance with his high school love. Because of a matchmaker. Finally, Jack found his special someone—Aimee—last fall. Again—"

"Let me guess. Because of a matchmaker."

He nodded. "Exactly. Don't you think there haven't been

hints—sometimes not-too-subtle hints—and attempts at matchmaking me since then?"

"If your family is reasonable, then we can simply explain why I'm here. Problem solved." She brushed her hands together to demonstrate that, then went over to the sink to start on the dinner dishes.

His work on his laptop continued as he spoke. "Sam, there's going to be an all-out barrage of people trying to get us together if they know you're here. They won't listen to our words. On top of that, three people have already tried."

She glanced up from the dishes. "You said two brothers had called."

"And Nathaniel."

"He wouldn't—"

"His wife and her sisters were the earlier matchmakers."

She pondered what he said as she rinsed out one of the pans and put it in the dishwasher. "I guess, then, that we need a legitimate reason for my being here. Something that isn't personal."

"Yes, if only we had some sort of business . . ."

She turned toward him with the pot scrubber in her hand. "I came here because I needed a—"

"Website," they said at the same time.

"But you don't have time to work on my website, so it doesn't make any difference."

"What I don't have time for is building a website from scratch. Scrapping your website and starting over with a one hundred percent custom one would take too long. But what if—" he turned his computer so that she could see "— we set up a pre-made website that comes with a shopping cart? We could get you up and rolling in a short amount of time. I can't fully customize it, but I can tweak it here and there so it looks like your brand with your colors and logo."

"It's that easy?"

He clicked around on sections of the page. "If you know what you're doing. And I do."

She grinned. "Does that mean I'll be back in business soon?"

"Definitely."

She glared at him. "I've already been here two days. Why didn't you do this before now?"

He looked sheepish. "My mind doesn't usually go here. I build websites from scratch. If a guest in your home said they'd like a hamburger and you didn't have any beef, would you suggest fast food?" Andy grinned. "Your look of horror answers the question. Same thing. There's nothing wrong with this site, it just isn't what I do. I also think it took impending doom for it to come to mind."

Sam laughed again. "You make it sound like you have a bunch of evil ogres in your family."

"No ogres. Just one mother who wants to see her baby happy."

Her eyebrow shot up.

"Her words. I'll give you good odds she'll say that when she's here tomorrow."

"You can't predict that."

"Can't I? How about you do the dishes while you're here if I'm right? It's my job if she doesn't."

She put out her hand to shake his, then realized it was soapy. Lowering her hand, she said, "Deal."

"Let's get to work."

Andy looked from Sam to his computer and frowned. "Why don't you come around here and stand beside me so you can tell me what you like and don't like as I build the site?"

Sam rinsed and dried her hands then did as he'd asked. "Do you usually do that with clients?"

Andy rolled his eyes. "I've never had a client in my house while working on the website, so no. Except my brother Jack."

Maybe being here made her like family to Andy. Why did that disappoint her?

"Picture your logo here." He pointed to the top left of the screen. "And we can change the colors. There are actually a fair number of options in here. I would normally give you a few choices to figure out what you wanted." He glanced at his watch. "But the clock is ticking. I need to have a viable website done before 11:00 a.m. tomorrow when my family arrives. I have to have a good enough start on it that your reason for being here is credible and truthful."

She liked that he wanted to be honest. If only Steven had shared his scruples.

He spent a few minutes on his computer, then spun it around so she could see it. "Okay. I tried this. What do you think?"

Her heart sank. A website with a fraction above zero personality was on the screen. "I don't know how to word this, Andy, but—"

He spun the computer back around. "Boring as dirt, isn't it?"

Relief washed through her. "I'm sorry, but it is. I don't necessarily need or even want animals, mutant or otherwise, dancing on the screen, but it has to be playful and fun. Dog owners are on my site because they want to make their beloved pets happy. They're going over and above."

Andy closed his eyes. For a moment she thought he was upset with her, but when he kept a calm expression on his face, she realized he was just thinking. When he opened his eyes, he immediately started typing on the computer. As he did so, Sam thought about the next twenty-four hours. She had no vehicle, and everything was frozen solid outside, so there was really nowhere she could go beyond the backyard.

Gracie wandered over and sat next to her, and she absentmindedly scratched her behind her ears. When Gracie leaned against her leg, Sam asked, "Would you like to go outside?" A soft *woof* greeted her. She got up from the stool and went over toward the door for her coat and boots. Andy was focused so intently on his computer screen that he didn't flinch. Even when she had to test the light switches to find which one turned on the outdoor lights, and the light over him blinked out for a second, he didn't slow down.

When she was fully clothed in her winter gear, she opened the door and they went outside. She walked Gracie away from the house to a good place for her to do her business and thought about the situation she'd gotten herself into. If she had a website—and it looked like there was a very good chance that she could have one in the next day or two —then she was back in business.

She could send out an email to all the customers on her list and let them know they could order again online. So many had just stopped ordering when the site stopped working. The problem was that she didn't know if this was too little too late to save Goodness Gracie! Only time would tell. Maybe she could add a new product line to Goodness Gracie! Something different . . .

Gracie returned to her side and trotted happily back toward the front door.

When they stepped inside, Andy said, "Thank goodness! I didn't know where you'd gone. I looked down the hall and couldn't find you."

Sam laughed. He was oblivious to everything. "Gracie needed to go outside. How's it going on the website?" At his blank expression, she pointed toward his computer.

He turned and raised his hands in the air in a shrug. "Sorry. Of course, the website."

She stepped forward. "Is something wrong, Andy?"

"Yes. No." He rubbed his hand over his face. "I need to be clear on what you need and want for your site. Let's go over to the couch." He picked up his computer and led the way.

They sat next to each other on the couch, Sam doing her best to not lean toward Andy when the cushion sank in that direction. This might have been a bad idea. Andy had his hand braced on the cushion to his right, so he also seemed to be trying to lean in the other direction.

"Maybe we should go to my office after all."

Sam turned toward him at the same time he looked her direction and felt the couch pulling her that direction.

He turned back toward his computer and she straightened, this time bracing her feet on the ground to fight the couch's desire for them to be closer. The move to his office apparently forgotten, Andy cleared his throat and said, "Tell me what you like about the website so far. Then tell me what you don't like."

"Your ego can't take the downside first?"

He chuckled. "It actually helps me work if we start with the good stuff."

She'd been joking with him, but now that she really looked at the design, she knew he still hadn't captured her business's fun and happiness. Sam pointed at the bright green he'd used at the top of the site. "I like that color."

When she stayed silent, he looked toward her. She chewed her lip as she stared at his laptop.

"Is that the only thing you like, Sam?"

She nodded. "I'm sorry. The design feels more . . . businesslike."

"You own a business. Am I right?"

"But I'm selling to dog owners. This isn't business to business. This is business to customer."

Andy stared at the screen. "You're right. I am so sorry. The last two sites I built, in fact, everything I've worked on for the last two months or more, has been for businesses selling to other businesses. They were supposed to deliver content in an attractive and appealing way."

"But no fun, huh?"

"Each of those sites was purposefully devoid of fun." He reached out into the air as though he were grabbing something and set it on top of his head. "I'm putting on my fun hat now."

Sam loved it that he could be silly while he worked.

"This will be the most fun dog treat site known to man or beast. Let's start with what you had before." He brought up the old site. "Are these the colors you told him to use?"

"Sort of. And you have to understand that the website actually worked, and it was cute when he built it."

He went to her current site and stared at his computer screen. "That seems to be an impossibility based on what's in front of my eyes."

"No, really."

"Do you have any idea about what happened to it?" he asked incredulously.

CHAPTER TEN

"This is a story of love found and lost."

Andy turned to Sam and found laughter simmering in her eyes. "Maybe I should add that I just need the facts and not the dramatics."

She shrugged. "That actually was the unvarnished truth. My mother met a graphic designer when she was at a resort in Arizona. Mom had lost Dad a year earlier. That might be long enough for some to heal, but she was still grieving deeply. Mom had fun on her trip. She enjoyed meeting new people and making friends, but she didn't want a relationship. In fact, she didn't even realize he was reaching out for one."

"I know that I have Holly's romance novels over on my bookshelf—" he pointed that direction "—but that doesn't mean I read romances. Is there a way to get to the heart of the story without this?"

She laughed. "This is the heart of this story. I know this is out of most men's normal realm of interest or comfort zone, but I think you need this background to understand why I have mutant animals on my website."

He waved his hand in a gesture that told her to continue.

"So anyway, Mom told him about her daughter and her daughter's business. He said he did websites professionally, and she got excited. She said, 'Oh my goodness, my Sam needs a new website.'"

This time Andy laughed. "I spent enough time around your mother on her visits to Lou that I can see hear her saying those exact words."

"She actually called me from the resort to tell me about this amazing, well-known web designer."

"Okay, so I understand that he is a supposed expert. But you had a website until he worked on it. Yes? Was that how you were selling the dog treats?"

"I built one myself on one of those free sites."

Andy cringed.

"I knew it wasn't great. Lou's wife is an artist and I talked her into making a new one. It looked better and served its purpose. That's what I had until this one."

"So this man built a website for free because he was interested in your mom?"

"Ha! If it had been free, this would be a very different tale I'm telling. He charged his full rates. But I looked him up first. He had great references, and I loved the other work he'd done. I knew he could build a website that would take my business to the next level. And it did."

Andy tapped the side of his computer. "But not this?"

"Nothing like this. My income exploded in the next six months. I established a contract with a commercial kitchen to manufacture the dog treats, and worked my tail off." She looked down at Gracie who was sitting there wagging hers. "No offense to the canine tail."

Gracie woofed.

"Everything was rainbows and roses. He made minor tweaks to the site to make it more functional as he and Mom dated. They lived about an hour apart from each other in Idaho, so the romance seemed to flourish. At least in his eyes."

"Hold it. I thought your mom wasn't interested in romance."

"She wasn't. But Mr. Clueless didn't seem to realize that. He brought her flowers. She thanked him. He took her to dinner. She thanked him. She made dinner for him, and he seemed quite happy about that. And then one day it all came crashing down."

"She told him no when he asked her out?"

"Worse." She closed her eyes for a moment and then opened them again. "He asked her to marry him."

"Whoa, whoa, whoa. He went from an occasional dinner out to a proposal?"

"Down on one knee with a diamond ring in his hand."

He winced. "My guess is the whole situation didn't turn out very well."

She sighed. "He was deeply wounded when she told him no. He sulked and repeated his proposal a week later. When she rebuffed him again, his sorrow turned to anger. What you have before you is the result. The website he'd built for the daughter was the one thing that he could take his frustration out on."

"Let me understand this. A respected designer, a professional in the industry that I am in, trashed your website because your mother wouldn't marry him?"

She tapped the end of her nose. "Got it in one."

"Now that I know his motivations, I understand more clearly what happened. He went deeply into the code of this website, and I haven't been able to figure out what he did to stop it from functioning."

"I woke up one morning, checked my sales, and didn't have any. I couldn't figure out why until I found an email from one of my clients saying my website looked strange. Of course, I thought, 'Strange how? It's just a website, right?' When I looked at it, I may have screamed. Maybe even loudly."

"It isn't just ugly; it's completely sabotaged. You have every right to sue him if you choose to."

"I'm not going there. I simply need a new one."

"Why didn't you build another basic one like you started out with?"

"The other one was too simple for my larger business. And every designer I contacted was too busy or too expensive. I *was* trying to learn to make a new site. Videos. Remember?"

Andy looked at the screen and clicked a few more times, almost as if to convince himself that it really was as bad as it seemed. "Do you have all the login information to the place where you bought the domain name? You bought it yourself, right?"

"Yes."

"Well, let's be grateful for that. I'll get you something that at least functions."

She lunged at him and hugged him. "Thank you so much, Andy."

When he turned his head to speak, her face was inches from his. He looked into Sam's brown eyes. Dark, chocolate brown that he could lose himself in. He reached up and covered her cheek with his hand and rubbed it with his thumb. She leaned into his hand and then forward toward him.

When he could feel Sam's breath on his lips and knew, finally, he was going to kiss her, an orange furball soared by him and landed on her lap.

Sam leaned back on the couch and stared into the face of his cat. "Lucy?"

He leaned back in his seat, breathing heavily. Struggling to catch his breath, he waited a moment before replying. "She doesn't usually jump on a stranger's lap. I think she might have been..."

"Jealous?"

"I didn't want to say it. But yes, you're in her domain. She was my first cat. She's welcomed all the additions, but still..."

He suddenly realized the mistake he'd almost made. There couldn't be any romance between them. Lori had *broken* his heart. The last time he'd seen her in town, pain had surged through him. Staying single remained his only option. Andy cleared his throat. "Yes, we'll get your website up and running very quickly. If not by tomorrow before they come, in the next couple of days."

"She's purring!" Sam grinned. "I've never felt this before. There's something soothing about it."

Lucy had definitely warmed up to Sam. Lori had tolerated the two cats he'd had when they'd dated. Lucy had seemed much happier when Lori stopped visiting.

"I don't know a whole lot about dogs. We had dogs and cats growing up, but for some reason, I always gravitated toward the cats. A couple of years ago, my brothers even got me a T-shirt at Christmas that said 'Crazy Cat Man' and had a dozen cats sitting beside someone who looked surprisingly like me." Kitty jumped up beside him.

Samantha pointed to his computer. "So, the old website is going to be taken care of? No one will ever know it existed?"

He gave a firm nod. "I'm going to do that in about five minutes. Give me your login information and we're good on that."

Not to be outdone, his other two cats came over, and Gracie trotted behind her new friend, Petunia. Andy picked up his pregnant cat and held her close for a moment before setting her down again. He wanted her to feel loved in his house.

"My family will get here about eleven, so I have very few hours to get your website up and running." His family. *Lunch.* He jumped to his feet. "How did we forget that I have to provide lunch tomorrow?" He raised his hands in frustration.

"How did *you* forget? I don't know what your family usually do for these lunches." She petted Lucy. "Maybe I'm a cat person after all." Gracie jumped up on the cushion beside her and snuggled close. "Well, cat and dog."

His frustration grew. "You seem very calm. We have to make a meal for eleven people tomorrow, maybe more if other family members can come at the last minute. With my mom, you never know. She might even invite the neighbors."

Sam laughed.

Andy's frustration ramped up.

"Andy, calm down. You're going to burst something. A year ago, I was making food for hundreds of people every day. A meal for a dozen is about as easy as it gets."

His shoulders relaxed, and then they ratcheted up again. "You were complaining earlier about the lack of fresh produce. I'm not going to drive out on this road after dark unless it's an emergency. Not in the winter."

"I haven't done a deep dive into your cupboards. I just looked on the surface. Do you have anything interesting in there?"

"Define 'interesting'?"

She started to speak and then stopped. "Let me ask first, are there any food allergies or major preferences I need to keep in mind?"

"No. My family eats pretty much anything, and we thankfully don't have any allergies to watch out for. I have a large freezer in the garage. It's where I keep the fish, berries, and any produce I froze from the summer."

She nudged the cat off of her lap and stood. "So, I complained about the lack of produce, and you didn't see a reason to tell me you had frozen produce?"

"Frozen isn't fresh. I'm not a chef. I didn't know you'd see them as the same."

"Fair enough. Let's go see what you've got, big boy." She chuckled as she walked away. "Andy, I am used to working in a man's world. For some reason, women are expected to cook in a home. Sure, there are men who do that, but that isn't the norm, and it's thought of as a wonderful perk when the man can cook. In the professional kitchen, male chefs still run the show. I had to do more than them to prove myself. That's made me highly adaptable."

He led the way out to the garage, closing the door so none of the cats could come out, but Gracie raced through as it shut. She was apparently used to going everywhere Sam went.

He lifted the lid on a massive chest freezer, stood back, and gestured toward it with his hand. "You're welcome to anything you find in there. I also have an assortment of flours. And I keep extra eggs in the spare refrigerator."

She glanced around the garage. "You have a spare refrigerator? You're one person."

"I'm one person right now, but in the summer, my house, which has an amazing dock out into the lake, can be busy. I almost always have family or friends here on a weekend. I also stay home a lot, and I like to cook, so I go through more food than the average single person."

Sam dug through the freezer, finding frozen blueberries, strawberries, rhubarb, and cranberries in one section. In another, she discovered green beans, broccoli, cauliflower, and peas. There were probably more things buried beneath those. Then she got to the seafood section. She found salmon, halibut, cod, and shrimp. "What, no king crab?"

Andy shuddered. "I don't think king crab survives freezing."

The man knew his seafood. She usually covered previously frozen king crab with a sauce. "I agree." She rooted around some more. "Now I've gotten to chicken and beef. Did you buy half a cow or something?"

"A quarter. I knew someone who raised beef to sell, and it's quite tasty."

So she'd literally landed in a chef's heaven by accident. "Are all these berries wild?"

"Only the cranberries, blueberries, and mossberries."

She'd never heard of mossberries. She'd have to look that one up. Samantha straightened and rubbed the small of her back. "Do you have other dry goods like pasta?"

"In the pantry inside."

"The pantry? How did I miss that?"

"It's through the doorway at the far end of the kitchen."

"I thought that led to a powder room, and I'd been using the one down the hall, so I didn't bother with it."

He grinned. "Please don't do that in there."

Laughing, she said, "I'll remember that. Now, I think we have everything we need to make a meal. I can do that while you work on my website."

"Sounds fair. If I have time, I'll take a break to come out and help."

Sam knew she could make this meal with one hand literally tied behind her back. But she'd enjoy working with Andy.

She stared at the loaded freezer. "Do you want homey foods or things that are more exotic?"

"Homey. You can test the exotic ones out on me while you're still here."

She chuckled. "Deal."

"What did you have in mind?"

"Well, I can cook almost any type of food that you can imagine. I've worked in a four-star restaurant in Europe, a barbecue place in Texas, and a cool little fusion restaurant in Los Angeles. We did Latin- and Asian-inspired foods." At his grimace, she said, "You'd be surprised at how tasty a burrito is with a sweet soy sauce dip."

"Let's stick to the more expected for my family."

"I most recently worked at the seafood restaurant. Would they want fish and shellfish?"

"Definitely."

"The good news about seafood is that it thaws very quickly. We don't have enough time to thaw a roast."

"I caught most of that myself last year, and I like the taste of summer in the winter."

"That is something I will probably never get used to." At his questioning expression, she said, "That March is winter. Everywhere else I've lived, March is spring. Flowers are blooming and everybody's happy because winter's over. In Alaska, we go ahead and run the longest dog sled race in the world because most of Alaska is still frozen solid."

Andy laughed. "You have a point there. When I was in college in Oregon, I enjoyed being able to get out at all times of the year."

She stopped and looked at him. "Then why did you move back to Alaska? You didn't even go back to the same place you grew up in. At least, that's my impression."

"You're right about that. I grew up in Juneau."

"I haven't been there or any other place in the Southeast yet. Only locations I can drive to. I didn't even have time for that when I worked in the restaurant."

"As to why I left, I missed the feel of Alaska. There's an openness, a friendliness, a quietness. Don't get me wrong, I enjoyed Oregon, and it was a nice place to live. I suppose if I'd had a good reason to stay, I would have. But Mom and Dad moved here to the Kenai Peninsula, and each time I visited I liked it more."

She grabbed one package each of salmon, halibut, and shrimp. She still wasn't sure what she'd do with the seafood, but she'd figure something out. "Here, hold these." She dropped them in his arms, then she grabbed an assortment of vegetables.

"My turn. Why are you in Alaska?"

She stopped moving. She could make it look all shiny and bright, or she could give him the unvarnished truth. The truth won. "A man. He moved to Alaska, said how awesome it was, and I moved here too." When she realized he was watching her with a curious expression, she added, "To my own apartment. But he said we would get engaged if I moved here, and we did."

"You keep speaking about him in the past tense, so I assume you're not together any longer."

Did she dare hope that Andy wanted to know that for personal reasons? "I think he liked the idea of a relationship more than he liked being in one. I thought it was because I was so busy with my job. People don't realize that chefs work a lot of hours." She looked up and into his eyes. "And I mean *a lot* of hours. On top of that, we had a saying in the first restaurant I worked at that 'a restaurant is only as good as the last meal you had there.' We have to be on point all the time and that adds another layer of stress."

She stood there with the frozen foods in her arms, not realizing until her skin started to go numb. She closed the lid on the freezer. "Long story short, the relationship problem wasn't my job."

She could still picture her glee when she had told Steven she was leaving her restaurant job to do her business full time. That they'd have more time together and could get married. And then he'd said he liked the relationship exactly as it was. Couldn't they leave things that way?

"I handed him back his ring." She hurried into the house.

Andy stared at Sam's back as she went into the house. She'd broken up with this man, Steven, just like Lori had broken up with him. Maybe Steven had been equally hurt. Inside the kitchen, he found that she had put all the frozen goods into the fridge to thaw, and was already standing in the pantry looking at what was in there.

"Heaven. I have gone to Heaven." She turned toward him. "I must have hit my head a lot harder than I thought I did when my SUV went into the ditch."

He stepped forward. "Are you feeling okay?"

"I don't know. Is this all really here?" She waved her hand at the shelves.

"It's all real. Why would you even question that? It's just a pantry."

Samantha giggled, but that quickly turned into laughter that rolled from her. She leaned her hand on one of the shelves to support herself. "Are you kidding? I don't think there is anywhere on earth a chef could be more thrilled to find herself stuck in." Pulling herself together, he saw the professional chef appear as she studied the shelves. "Would seafood lasagna be too exotic for your family?"

He mulled that over. "It's all familiar ingredients, so it should be fine."

"I can make the pasta in the morning."

He pointed toward the far corner of the pantry. "I'm sure I have lasagna noodles there."

She turned toward him and raised one eyebrow.

"Okay, the chef wants to make her own pasta, is that what you're telling me?"

She grinned. "I do. It also gives me something to do, and I noticed you have a pasta machine here. In fact you probably have every gadget and appliance known to modern man."

"Guilty as charged. Part of that's not my fault, though. My family knows I enjoy cooking and they've gotten together before to buy me things like that. The pasta machine was for Christmas three or four years ago."

"It's high quality. Do you use it?"

"I do. I made some chicken noodle soup a few weeks ago and brought that baby out for the noodles."

Sam rolled her eyes. "Heaven, I tell you. Heaven." He even had semolina flour, so she wouldn't have to substitute regular flour.

Sam turned to leave the pantry and Andy stepped back so they wouldn't touch. It would be best if he kept his distance from her. He followed her into the kitchen.

"I'll get to work on this meal first thing in the morning."

Andy gasped as he pictured his family arriving and lunch being far from ready. "Tomorrow? Not tonight? Eleven people."

Grinning, she said, "I'm a chef. I have plenty of time to do this in the morning. If you focus on my website tonight, maybe you can help me then."

Happiness surged through him at the mention of them working together and that concerned him. "I'd like that. One thing we probably should think about in advance, though, is dessert."

For the first time since he'd mentioned lunch, Sam appeared uncertain. She opened the fridge. "I'm hoping something will inspire me. That's the flaw in my plan. I'm not a pastry chef. I can turn out something decent, though."

"I don't think my family expects anything beyond that."

"Didn't I hear something about Holly being a genius with pies, but that she wasn't coming?"

At his nod, she said, "Then they are used to pretty high-quality stuff. You work on the website and I'll do some research for dessert. Deal?"

"Deal."

CHAPTER ELEVEN

*S*am grabbed her laptop and started to search through dessert recipes. She needed to make something delicious. She just wasn't as comfortable baking as she was cooking.

She'd noticed that Andy had an ice cream maker in his pantry, so she could make something with the berries in his freezer. Even though Alaskans didn't seem to care about the time of year when they ate ice cream or the ambient air temperature—she'd seen them go out for ice cream in twenty below zero weather—she didn't love that.

She knew exactly who to ask about this dilemma. She picked up her phone and hit her most-used speed dial number. "Mom!"

"How are you doing, honey?"

How was she? She was about to lose her business. Maybe that wasn't true anymore. Andy was fixing her website. Repairing her SUV would probably take most, if not all, of the rest of her savings. But a functioning website would allow orders to start coming in. It looked like she was going to make it. At least she hoped so.

"Great. How are you?"

Silence greeted her.

"Mom? Are you okay?"

"I'm fine. But that was the most pathetic *great* I've ever heard. What's going on up there in the frozen north?"

So that hadn't gone as planned. "Well, I think everything is going to turn out good." She forced as much enthusiasm as she could into that sentence.

"What on earth has happened? Do I need to get the next flight out of here?"

"No. Everything's fine. Don't worry."

"Then you'd better start explaining right now, Missy, or I *will* be on my way to the airport. I know you don't have a big apartment, but you can find space for me on the couch."

"Well, I'm not there right now. My business had a little bit of a setback."

She had stupidly forgotten that she hadn't told her mother about what had happened with her website. She never should have made this call. "You see, Mom, Herb was upset at you when you turned down his proposal. Especially when you turned him down the second time he asked."

"I don't understand. What does that have to do with your business? You seem to be hinting that it does."

Sam looked heavenward. *How do I do this?* Gracie came over and jumped up beside her. She made one of her medium barks.

"Is that my Gracie?"

Sam laughed. "She must have known we were talking on the phone." Had that been a big enough distraction so she could move on to cake recipes?

"Start explaining what's going on."

No, it hadn't. "Well, my website stopped functioning."

"You mean it stopped working and he wouldn't fix it? I guess I can understand that. But you paid for it, so he should have."

Sam sighed. "No, Mom. He made the website not function. And those cute animals that were on it . . ."

"Those dogs were adorable. I was impressed that he could do that."

"So was I. He's very talented. He was able to turn those adorable dogs into creatures that look like mutant zombie animals. Nothing on the website works either. All you get is a single page with crazy animals."

Once again silence greeted her, but only for a few seconds, and then her mom asked, "Are you kidding me? A grown man did that to a paying client because he had his affections spurned by the client's mother?"

That about summed it up. "That seems to be the case."

"Why that—" she all but growled over the phone. "I can't believe I was even considering going out with that man again. Never. Do you need financial help, Sam? Is that why you called?"

"Mom, I would never ask you for money. Not unless I was absolutely desperate."

"I'm here for you." This was the most normal she'd heard her mom in over a year. Maybe Herb had helped her come out of the bubble of grief she'd been walking around in.

"I just realized you said you're not home. Did you lose your home?"

"No, Mom, it's fine. My marketing guy—you remember Nathaniel? You met him and his wife when you were visiting last summer."

"Such a cute couple. And that baby! Oh my goodness! Absolutely adorable." Her mother had been in town when Nathaniel had held a barbecue for his clients.

"Well, Nathaniel recommended a web designer."

"I hope this one isn't another Valentino."

Sam laughed. "I remember Grandma using that name."

"He was a screen star in the silent movie days. But don't think you're distracting me. What's going on, Sam? Tell me the truth."

"The designer that Nathaniel recommended first turned me down. Nathaniel had said he thought he would be afford-able, even though he had a high level of expertise. He also said he was kind. Nathaniel's sister-in-law is married to this man's brother, so he's family of a sort. Anyway, I drove down to Kenai and knocked on his door. He told me he was too busy to take on any new clients."

"The nerve of that man when you'd done all that."

"No, Mom. I've actually seen that he is busy. But as I drove away, I decided to go back and ask him one more time, to plead with him. Because my business was going to go down the drain if he didn't help or unless somebody he knew could help. Then I hit an ice patch on the road."

Her mother gasped. "You sound fine and I know Gracie's there with you. Did you just slide off the road?"

"Yes and no. We slid off the road onto a rock. My SUV's in the shop right now getting checked out."

"And where are you?"

That was the million-dollar question, wasn't it? "I'm staying with the web designer. I had the accident down the road from him and it's fairly remote here. Otherwise, I'd have to fly home, and then I'd have to come back to get the vehicle when it's repaired. He has a separate wing of the house that he built for guests, so that's where I am at night. It's just Gracie and me behind a locked door. Oh, and a cat door for his cats."

"Cats and a dog?"

Leave it to her mom to ask that question instead of delving deeper and deeper into the sleeping arrangements. She loved that her mother trusted her judgment. "Gracie seems to be quite happy about the cats. But only one of them has decided that she is a creature it wants to spend any time near. It's a pregnant cat, and they seem to be becoming buddies.

"And, Mom, you're going to be amazed. He's Andy O'Connell."

"Wait. I know one man with that name—Lou's friend from college."

"That's the one."

"Had you kept in touch with him?"

"I barely knew him." But she'd wished he had noticed her.

"What did your brother have to say about your being there?"

She winced. "I hope he doesn't find out while I'm here. You know how protective he is of 'his baby sister.'"

Her mother chuckled. "You may be right about that."

"Oh, and I also called to see if you have any idea for something I can make for a dessert. You know that is not my specialty. There's a family lunch every week and they're all coming to his house tomorrow. The main course is easy because he has the most stocked fridge, freezer, and cupboards I've ever seen outside of a commercial kitchen. But dessert . . ."

"His family is coming?"

"Yes," Sam said slowly.

Sam could hear peals of laughter through the phone. "Mom?"

"Just—" she gasped. "A minute." After a long wheezing breath, her mother said, "You are going to be on the hot seat. Is his mother coming?"

"Yeah. But I'm only a client."

"Oh, honey. Mothers don't care. It has been years since I've seen him. Is he reasonably attractive?

He'd made her young heart go pitter patter. "He has reddish hair, green eyes, and a beard."

"He sounds like a lumberjack."

Sam laughed. "No, he's a handsome geek version of that."

"Handsome, huh? Is he available? The bigger question is, are you interested?"

She and her mother had always had a relationship that was closer to sisters, probably because Sam's sisters were all older and it had just been her at home by the time she got to high school. "Mom, focus. Dessert."

"Well, you can't blame a mother for asking."

"Actually, you can. Dessert, *please?*"

"Your Aunt Gertie's spice cake is always a hit. That's a very straightforward recipe with basic ingredients."

It didn't matter if it was basic or exotic. This man probably had the ingredients here somewhere. "I remember everybody loving that cake. What kind of frosting did she use, though? I can't quite picture it."

"Sometimes she used spice frosting. Sometimes plain vanilla. If you're ready, I can read you the recipe." It would have been simpler for her mother to scan the recipe and email or message it to her, but her mom was the opposite of a techie.

"I'm ready."

Sam wrote down the recipe, and they talked for a few more minutes, then said their goodbyes.

When Andy came out of his office about an hour later, he sniffed the air as he walked. "I thought you said you didn't bake. That smells fabulous."

"I hope your family likes spice cake."

"Sam, my family is very easy to please, especially when it comes to desserts."

"It's almost ready to come out of the oven. It's Aunt Gertie's special recipe."

"If that tastes even half as good as it smells, I want to thank Aunt Gertie."

She laughed. "It's actually my grandmother's Aunt Gertie. If you can think of a way to thank her at this point, since she's been gone for a very long time—"

"Okay. I can thank your mother, then."

She stared at this man. He was . . . nice. He seemed to be exactly who she thought he was. But was anyone who you thought they were?

The timer went off, and she pulled the cake out of the oven. After testing it, she determined it was done and set it on a rack to cool. "Well, that's all I need to do tonight." She set the potholders down and turned toward him. "Is it too soon to ask how my website's going?"

"Actually, this site with a built-in shopping cart is working very nicely." He looked contrite. "I'm sorry I didn't think of this before. I'm sorry about a lot of things, Sam."

"Not your fault. I expected too much from a virtual stranger. And a busy one at that. As soon as you get that website running, I'll start posting on social media and send out a newsletter to see if I can save my business."

This was a strong woman. He didn't think she would ever choose something simply because it was the easy path.

Lori had broken up with him instead of trying to make things work. A little voice asked, *Was that really what Lori did?* The last time he'd seen her—a chance encounter at the grocery store—she had seemed far happier than she had ever been with him. But that didn't erase the pain in the center of his heart that he got every time he thought about Lori. The love of his life.

Sam turned off the oven and looked around the kitchen. The kitchen she had left spotless. "I think I'm going to head to bed now and read. I'll set my alarm for five so I can get started on the meal. Is that okay with you?"

Andy clenched up at the thought of an alarm that early. "Night owl here. I was planning to work for a while longer on your site and go to bed considerably later than this."

Sam bit her lip. "I need to have enough time to get the meal ready. I always allow enough time that I'm comfortable and not feeling rushed in any way. I could, of course, whip something up faster if it was less complicated."

"Your menu sounds great. If you don't mind me sleeping while—"

"What if I wake you up by working in the kitchen?"

"Not a chance. Two things: one is that I sleep like a rock. A rock with four cats draped over it."

She laughed. Andy loved seeing her eyes light up. *Push away those thoughts, O'Connell.*

"Two: I actually insulated some of the interior walls. I wanted my guests to be able to get up earlier or stay up later than me and not have sound transfer from one room to the next. In the house we grew up in, that was difficult because there were five boys not too far apart in age. Can you imagine the noise we could make?"

She laughed. "There were five of us, but four were girls. Our big issue was getting time in the bathroom."

"Dad's rule was that we had to be quiet on Saturday morning so Mom could sleep in. She had a state job she worked at part-time and loved to sleep in on Saturday."

"I'll use my inside voice, as my brother Lou is teaching his toddler to do. And I'll be as quiet as I can be when it comes to pots and pans."

"And I'll try to finish in time to help. Will you need me to do anything in particular in the morning?"

Sam shrugged. "I want help with all of it in particular. I'll give you good directions."

Sam said that in a way that made him happy to work with her. She must have been a popular head chef. "I can be your sous chef. Once I've had breakfast, of course."

"Of course. Is there anything special you'd like?"

"Hash browns, two eggs over easy, and bacon."

"Done."

"Sam, I was kidding. You don't have to fix me breakfast. I can do it myself. I'll probably just grab a bowl of cereal so we don't interrupt what we're working on for lunch."

"No. I can do that for you." She pushed off from the counter. "I'll see you whenever you get up. Gracie?" The dog trotted over. "Ready for a walk?"

He looked from the dog to the door.

"Sam, it's kind of late to be going outside for a walk. And cold. And very, very dark. With wild animals."

"We always call it a walk. I'm just going to go outside far enough from the door so she doesn't mess up the snow there, and we'll be right back."

She put her coat, boots, and hat on, leashed up her dog, and went outside.

She may have been born in another state, but Samantha Santoro certainly fit in here. And he liked that quality far more than he wanted to.

CHAPTER TWELVE

*W*hen Sam went to bed, she tossed the clothes she'd worn into a laundry basket in the closet. She had one set of clean clothes now, so she'd wash them again tomorrow morning to stay on top of the situation.

She slid under the sheets. This man thought of everything. The soft bedding with a fluffy comforter covered a bed that was just right. After reading a short time, she turned out the light.

It felt like minutes later when she rolled over and pulled the covers up to her chin, snuggling down into the bed. Peering at the clock, she saw it was an hour before she needed to get up.

A wet nose touched hers.

"Gracie, settle down and let Mom sleep a little longer." Sam snuggled deeper into the covers and pulled them around her.

Gracie swiped her tongue across Sam's cheek. She'd taken

her out last night right before they went to bed, so she shouldn't need a potty break.

"What is it, Gracie?" she murmured. Sam felt herself relaxing and slipping into sleep again.

Gracie barked once.

It wasn't her usual soft *woof*, so Sam opened her eyes. "Okay, I'm listening now. What do you need?"

Gracie whimpered.

Sam set up on the edge of the bed. As soon as she did, Gracie trotted over to the closet. Sam slid her feet into her slippers and walked over to see what had interested her dog.

The laundry basket now contained an exhausted-looking Petunia and four tiny kittens. The mother cat and her babies all seemed to be okay. But what did she know about cats? Sam checked the time, knowing this was much earlier than she should wake up Andy after a late night of work. He'd need his energy when his family came later.

Sam searched on her phone for information about cats giving birth. According to what she read, everything seemed okay. Petunia opened her eyes and started bathing one of the kittens.

"Okay, so you're just resting after all your work? Is that it, new mom?"

Sam found an article on the postnatal care of the mother and her kittens, and it said the room needed to be warm. She'd find the thermostat and turn the heat up. It also said she needed to have everything for her needs nearby—food, water, and a cat box. She'd bring those in too.

Sam scratched Gracie's ear. "I guess she felt safe here with me and you, Gracie. Didn't you, Petunia?"

The new mom finished licking that baby and moved on to the next one.

"You're going to need a better set-up than a bed of my clothes." Sam put her hand on her mouth. "My clothes," she said with a sigh. "I brought a single other outfit. Now I have one outfit, don't I, Petunia? Not that I begrudge you that. You found the thing that looked most like a nest and that's where you had your babies."

Sam went into the attached bathroom, took a shower, and came out to find Gracie still standing at the closet door like a nervous parent. Sam put yesterday's clothes back on. Maybe later, she could spend a couple of hours in a robe while her clothes washed. It might also be worth a try to see if the others were salvageable. Leaning closer to the new kitten's bed, she grimaced. "Maybe not." She picked up her phone again to search for more new birth information. "Gracie, we need to give her a clean bed."

Sam opened the door. "Come on, Gracie."

Gracie sat and looked from Sam to the new mom and back, but she didn't leave her post.

"Walk?" She had never once known her dog to turn down a walk. That got her a low whimper, but Gracie stayed put. "Okay, I'll leave the door open for you."

Sam made a bowl of food for Petunia, then brought that and a bowl of water to the closet. After that, she went to the room with the cat boxes, but didn't know if each belonged to a specific cat. She'd have to wake Andy up after all, but at least he'd gotten to sleep a little longer. She knocked on his bedroom door. Hearing nothing from inside, she knocked harder.

A barely recognizable man with tousled hair pulled the door open. Dressed in blue-plaid flannel pajama bottoms with a coordinating blue T-shirt, he looked adorable. *Don't fall for him, Sam.*

He squinted as he focused on her. "What's wrong?"

"Kittens." She pointed down the hall.

Andy went that direction. When he saw them, he grinned. "It's been years since I've had newborn kittens. Thank you for getting food and water. I'll get her box." He placed it on a towel in the closet. "We'll check on her every so often to make sure she's okay. And we'll have to keep everyone out of here today."

Once the mother cat and kittens were settled, Sam made the promised breakfast. Andy complimented her on it as he quickly ate it so he could get to work. A quick check on his phone had shown an email from a client that kept making changes to their website. They wanted these changes done immediately. He closed the door to his office minutes after she'd set the food in front of him, with the promise that he'd see her at lunchtime if not before.

CHAPTER THIRTEEN

*A*ndy worked to finish Sam's site as she made lunch for his family. As the time drew nearer, he realized that he could be at her side this morning—and he very much wanted to do that—or he could make more progress on the site she desperately needed. The opportunity to cook with her today slipped away.

As she'd promised, a lunch of seafood lasagna, roasted vegetables, and fresh bread awaited him when he came out of his office.

His parents were the first to arrive. Sam stood nervously in the kitchen, restlessly shifting from one foot to the other, with Gracie at her side. But the poor dog seemed to be conflicted because she kept looking between Sam and the newcomers she wanted to greet.

His mother, who carried a jug of iced tea, gave Andy a kiss on his cheek. He knew she couldn't come empty-handed. His dad closed the door behind them and hung up his jacket while his mother surveyed the room, her gaze stopping on Samantha. Her eyes widened, and a smile started, turning into a grin. "And who do we have here?"

He hated to quash the unmistakable happiness in her voice. But he definitely didn't want her getting the wrong idea.

"Mom, this is my *client* Samantha Santoro." His mother looked from Sam to him as she processed the information. He could see the wheels spinning in her head. Was she just a client? And even if she was, could she change that situation?

"Her website shut down and I'm trying to get it fixed."

His mother deflated at those words, but gracious as ever, walked over to Sam. "It's lovely to meet you, Samantha, wasn't it?"

Sam, much more reserved than she'd been around him in the last couple days, said, "Yes, ma'am. I'm grateful that your son is helping me with the website for my business."

"I see. I haven't known my son to have a client come to the family lunch before." She turned back toward him, her smile growing again.

"My client—" he was being very careful to not sound too cozy with his housemate "—had an accident as she left my place. She's staying here while her vehicle is repaired." As soon as the words were out of his mouth, he knew he'd made the biggest mistake of his life.

His mother's eyes popped open wider than before, something he would have never thought possible. "She's staying *here?*"

Andy gulped. This wasn't going to go well. He could feel that in his bones. "Yes, ma'am." When was the last time he'd called his mother *ma'am*?

"I see."

He wasn't sure what she saw, but he suspected it wasn't anything close to reality.

"Mom, she's staying in the other wing of the house. She's a client. She's going home to Anchorage to run her business as soon as her SUV is repaired."

There. Leaning back on his heels, he knew he'd explained the situation in a way that everyone should be able to understand. Even his mother, who seemed to be able to overreact to anything that could be a potential relationship for one of her sons.

His mother looked toward the door at the other side of the house. It did lock. He'd made sure of that when he'd built the house. He'd wanted his guests to feel like they had privacy. Only the cat door allowed free movement from one side to the other. He'd had to install that right after his first guests stayed here because his cats had freaked out about a closed door.

"Son, I'm not sure about this." His father's voice caught him off guard.

Andy whirled around toward his dad. Mom had decided it was okay, but Dad had not?

Samantha said, "I'm a guest, sir. If I were a male client, would you think anything more of this?"

His dad sighed. He mulled it over for a moment, then he said, "No. I wouldn't."

"I work in a man's world, sir. At least I used to. I'm a chef. Believe me, I can hold my own with one male computer designer."

Andy added, "And she's my college roommate's younger sister."

His mother smiled. "Lou's sister?" At his nod, she continued. "I'm glad you're helping her with her business. How is he doing?"

"He has a new baby."

She gave Andy a sweet expression. "Isn't that nice? He's happily married and has a baby."

"And twin toddlers."

Her eyebrows rose at that. "That's so nice. You need that life too." To Andy, she added, "I just want to see my baby happy."

Sam covered her mouth—he was sure to hide laughter because her eyes sparkled with it.

"Sam's a professional chef, so she made lunch."

His dad smiled at Sam. "I enjoy a good meal, so I'm even more pleased to meet you."

His parents were always kind, but it usually took his dad longer to warm up to newcomers than it did his mom. Sam had broken through immediately.

Gracie stepped away from Sam's side and came over to check out the newcomers. She went straight to his dad. Smart dog.

"And who do we have here?" His dad knelt to pet the dog, who now sat in front of him.

"That's Gracie. She loves all humans. Well, almost all humans. And she seems to like Andy's cats too. But only the pregnant cat likes her in return."

"The pregnant cat?" His mother looked around the room, her eyes stopping on the three felines lined up on the sofa.

Andy said, "Not pregnant anymore."

"Right! She had her kittens during the night."

He explained how Petunia had come to live here. "When I took her to the vet, I discovered we were about to have kittens."

"Gracie didn't want to leave her side earlier. She seems to be the doting aunt."

"We had a dog and cat that were like that when you were very little." His mother's brow furrowed as she thought about it. "Actually, I think you're too young to even remember. They loved each other. Do you think they would mind if we sat down?" His mom pointed at the couch covered in cats.

Andy laughed. "They won't mind, but will you mind having a cat on your lap ten seconds after you do?"

His mother chuckled as she walked across the room. "I'm looking forward to it. Where do you think you got your love of them from?"

Everyone arrived and settled in. Andy had to admit that having family here cheered his house up. He might have to do the lunch more often. A short time later, when his parents were on the couch talking to Rachel and Maddie, he motioned for his brothers to follow him. When they were all in his office, he leaned out the door and saw his parents still listening to their new daughters-in-law, so he closed the door.

He turned toward the men. "What have you done?"

Jack seemed confused, but Noah and Mark looked sheepish.

"About what?" Jack asked.

"Samantha. Here. What were you thinking?"

Adam sighed. "We wanted her to *call* you."

Mark, his oldest brother, said, "Exactly. It never occurred to us that she'd hop in her vehicle and drive to your place from Anchorage."

Noah added, "But it does show she's spunky."

Andy grinned. Sam definitely had spunk. He forced his focus back to the conversation. "That's beside the point. For years, we've fought Mom's matchmaking attempts. Then your wife, Adam, and her sisters got involved."

Noah said, "I'm grateful for that."

Mark sat on the edge of the desk and crossed his arms over his chest. "That makes two of us."

"Three. I'm grateful for their interference," Jack said. "I might have never met Aimee without their matchmaking."

Andy sighed. "You're missing the point!"

Adam put his hand on Andy's shoulder. "What is the point? Are you unhappy that she's here?"

Was he? "No. But I don't like people interfering in my life."

His brothers laughed.

Jack said, "Just accept it and everything will be fine."

Adam opened the door and his brothers filed out before Andy had solved the problem. But what *was* the problem? Maybe that he'd gotten used to her being here. At the very least, he needed to defuse the situation with his parents.

He picked up his laptop and brought it out to the kitchen island. "Hey, everyone, I want you to see this website that I'm working on for Samantha. My client." His family came over and crowded around. "It isn't one I normally do from scratch, it's kind of premade. But she needed something in a hurry to help get her business up and running."

"You have a new business, Samantha?" his mother asked.

"Not new, Mrs. O'Connell. My website stopped working. That's why Nathaniel sent me to Andy."

Nice touch, Sam, bringing in Nathaniel. She hadn't found him online and pursued him.

After checking out the website, Noah asked, "You make dog treats?"

Andy hadn't considered his brothers as customers for

Goodness Gracie! But Noah had a big dog who could probably eat a lot of treats in a day.

"I do. Gracie loves them." Her dog sat beside her with a sweet expression as she talked about her.

Adam said, "Hey, I've heard of Goodness Gracie! I hadn't put the pieces together until now. Emma loves those treats. Someone told us about them." He tapped the side of his head with his finger, then raised that finger in the air. "I remember now! My wife Holly—"

"The author. I love her books."

"I'll tell her that. Holly's sister Jemma told her about the treats. And Jemma's married to Nathaniel." He turned toward Noah. "You have got to get some of those treats. Emma thinks they're the best thing ever. And she'll behave really well in order to get one."

Adam asked Sam, "Do you have any of those here?"

Sam said, "No. Just the ones I've been testing."

"I'll take whatever you have."

"Okay. Remind me before you go. I tried a salmon version, but Gracie wanted nothing to do with it. The cats waited while they baked and gobbled them up."

They laughed. The timer went off on the lasagna, so Sam said, "Dinner will be ready in about fifteen minutes."

Andy headed for the pantry. "I'll get the plates and silverware ready."

"Great. With all these people, buffet style is the only thing that's going to work, isn't it?"

He smiled. "One of the reasons Mom and Dad bought their house was because it could fit a large dining room table. My table seats six and I rarely use it. A buffet lunch will be fine here." He made several trips and stacked up everything they'd need.

Lunch went better than she'd hoped. Everyone loved the lasagna. Aimee and Rachel both asked if she could give them step-by-step directions to make it. When everyone had eaten their fill—and some complained they'd eaten too much—she started to clean up, but Andy told her to sit down and relax while he took care of it.

CHAPTER FOURTEEN

*S*am chose a seat near Rachel, one of a cluster of chairs in the corner of the great room.

"What do you think of this giant family event?" Rachel asked.

Sam laughed. "I also have four siblings—three sisters and a brother—so I am definitely not intimidated by large family gatherings."

Rachel surveyed the room. "It took me a while. I don't come from a warm and fuzzy family situation. We didn't even get together for Thanksgiving the last few years. And Christmas, when you're in the retail industry, can be a bit of a rush."

"Well, I'm now in retail, but it's online. I don't think anybody told me, Rachel, what you do. As long as that's not too intrusive of a question from someone you just met."

Rachel laughed. "That's the first question asked in America, second only to 'What's your name?' I own a clothing store in downtown Anchorage."

Sam leaned forward. "Clothing? What kind? And how

was this very important bit of information left out from earlier conversations today?"

"You must be a fashion lover?"

"I'm a new fashion lover." At Rachel's curious expression, Sam continued. "I worked in restaurants all of my adult life. Fashion takes a backseat to comfort, and the hours are long, so you don't have time for recreational activities that require special clothing."

"You're doing the dog treat business now, though?"

"I quit my job, and I could not be happier. This—" she gestured toward the group around them "—is a fun event to cook for."

"Well, I wouldn't say there was no pressure to it."

Sam grinned. "There isn't any pressure when I don't have a connection to the people in the room. Andy's the super nice guy who let me stay here while my SUV was being fixed. He figured out a way to help save my business with a quick and simple new website, but there isn't any connection beyond that." She kept a happy smile on her face even though those words disturbed her.

Rachel turned toward their host. "He is nice. And handsome."

"He's definitely that." Sam agreed.

"Are you a fan of men with beards?"

Sam thought about it. Was she fond of men with beards? Only this bearded man. Not that she had anything against beards, per se, but it certainly looked good on Andy. She carefully answered, "Beards are fine on the right person." When Sam turned back toward Rachel, she realized she'd been watching her. "And I can go either way on men with reddish hair, but it does look good on him."

Rachel threw her head back with laughter. "Touché."

Sam said, "I think we can both agree without hesitation that Andy is handsome and nice. He also lives here and I live in Anchorage."

Rachel reached out and touched the bookshelves beside her. "Andy chose every bit of this. He'd finished building it not long before I met Noah. He was so thrilled with his results that, for months, he explained every detail each time I came here. It would take a lot to get him out of his home."

Sam's gaze slid back over toward Andy. She was glad she saw him as a friend and nothing more. She'd built a business that was headquartered in Anchorage, and after everything she'd been through with it lately, she did not want to try to lift it up and move it somewhere else, even just hours away.

Enough about Andy. "Did you see the kittens?"

Rachel shook her head. "I was told not to try to see them because we didn't want to bother the mother and because the dog had taken up guard duty."

Smiling, Sam said, "Gracie has decided she is Petunia's protector. But Gracie's my sweetie, so if you want to see the kittens, we can go."

Rachel's eyes lit up. "Noah has a dog, and I've grown to love Zeke, but I've wanted to have a cat since I was a child."

The two of them stood and walked over to Sam's side of the house.

As they started down the hall, Sam asked, "Your parents didn't like cats?" She looked toward her new friend and saw sad eyes.

"My parents didn't like much of anything." Rachel had a forced happy note in her voice when she said, "Except for their business. They loved their business." Rachel didn't elaborate, and Sam didn't ask any more questions.

Sam went into her bedroom first but didn't see Gracie.

"Where are you, Gracie?" A soft *woof* came from inside the closet. Sam stepped in and found Gracie curled up next to the basket with the kittens. "Are you helping, sweetie?"

Gracie had a content expression. Sam waved Rachel over. "I think you're fine if you stand here. Gracie is the sweetest dog to ever be on planet Earth, but she's definitely protecting this mom and her babies."

When Rachel moved next to Sam, Gracie lifted her head and watched her.

"She's with me, Gracie. It's okay." After a few more seconds, Gracie put her head back down. She gave one more soft *woof,* as though to let everyone know that she was in charge here.

Rachel knelt so she could be at the cats' level. "They are so tiny and adorable."

"I know. I had never been around cats before, but oh my goodness. They can't see or hear yet. They're totally dependent on their mom."

Rachel stood. "That's how I felt when our plane went down and Andy had to get us out of the wilderness."

Sam turned toward her. "Excuse me? I definitely did not hear that story."

"Then you haven't heard the story of how we met. I came to Alaska to find my brother, who we thought was in Talkeetna. Mrs. O'Connell asked me to play a practical joke on Noah at the same time she got him to fly me there. Everything seemed fine. We took off and were going in the right direction. It shouldn't have been a very long flight, and I never should have seen him again after that, but we had engine trouble and the plane went down."

Sam gasped. "You're both okay, so I guess it turned out all right."

"We ended up stuck in the wilderness for days."

"The two of you alone?"

Rachel laughed. "Don't think there was anything going on hanky-panky-wise. Noah was angry with me at first. We were just trying to get out of there in one piece."

"You and I should probably go back out and join the rest of the group before they start looking for us and upset the tiny kittens." Sam looked at Gracie. "You take good care of Petunia. And if you need to eat or go potty, come see me, okay?" Gracie thumped her tail on the floor.

As they went down the hall, Rachel said, "And when we were lost, there was Zeke, of course. He made an excellent chaperone."

Samantha grinned. "I can imagine that. But the two of you did decide to get married."

Rachel laughed. "Let's say that it was not love at first sight." Stepping out the door to the great room, Rachel glanced over at her husband with a sweet expression on her face. It was clear that it may not have been love at first sight, but it was definitely love. Rachel turned back toward Sam. "Anyway, this is a great time of year for me to relax and think about what's next."

"With what?"

"I forget that you're not part of the family, that you don't know every little thing about me. We got married on Valentine's Day."

A twinge at being the one unattached woman in the room hit her. "Congratulations!"

Rachel blushed. "Thank you. In addition to figuring out being married, I've learned that this is a slow season for my store. It's still winter, but no one wants more winter clothes.

And it's not quite spring, so pretty spring clothes aren't appealing."

Sam looked down at the pair of jeans she'd been wearing for days and then up at Rachel. "Speaking of being unappealing, I only have what I'm wearing and need more clothes. If I gave you the key to my apartment, would you choose some clothes and ship them here? You can tuck the key in the box."

"Sure. But I know you must have friends in Anchorage who know your taste."

Samantha shook her head. "My friends work in the restaurant business. They don't get much time off."

Rachel smiled. "Then I'm happy to do it."

"Besides, those who work in restaurants tend to be very casual. It's all about comfort in the back. I think you could actually coordinate something for me. I'd like to be more attractive." Sam wanted to take those words back the second she said them.

Her new friend raised an eyebrow, but didn't comment. "I hope I figure out your taste right. Is there anything else you need?"

Sam turned toward Andy. Her heart did its usual fast-paced beating when she looked at him. She'd quit trying to tell it to stop doing that because it hadn't worked.

Rachel turned to look in the same direction. "You've got your sights set on Andy. Don't you?"

Samantha whipped around toward Rachel. "No. Absolutely not. Bad idea."

Rachel sat in the chair she'd been in earlier and grinned. "I don't think even you believe that. He's taking a lot of razzing for you being here today."

Sam sighed as she sat. "I know. He told me that would

happen last night when we realized everyone was coming and I didn't have anywhere to go."

Rachel pursed her lips and appeared to be pondering the situation. "I could—"

Samantha held up one hand in a stop motion. "Please don't. So far, Nathaniel, Mark, and Adam have called to mention me to Andy."

Rachel winced.

"And then his family came today. There has been an endless stream of questioning glances."

Rachel said, "You got that right."

"I'm glad I wasn't the only one who noticed. At least they didn't say anything else about matching us up."

"That is a good thing. In the days Noah and I were in the wilderness, no one pushed us together. We both can see how that turned out." Rachel held up her left hand with her wedding ring sparkling on it.

"You met him because of an accident."

"I met him because of his mother. I got to know him because of an accident." She turned toward Sam and raised an eyebrow. "A bit like your situation, wouldn't you say?"

Sam rolled her eyes. "Don't any of you take a break from matchmaking?"

Laughing, Rachel shook her head. "Apparently not."

Mark's wife—what was her name?—walked toward them.

She pulled a chair over. "I know, Sam, that there are a lot of new faces and names here today. I'm Maddie."

"Whew! I am a little overwhelmed, so thank you."

These women were so nice. Andy was in a great family. Only Sam wasn't part of this family and she needed to remember that. She was a guest and would be here a very brief time.

Maddie pulled a chair over and sat down with them. "Sam, I have to tell you: that lunch was one of the best meals I've had in a really long time."

"Thank you. It was fun to make. Andy didn't have time to help with it, but he's helped me in the kitchen at other times."

"Did you work well together?" Maddie asked.

Rachel and Sam groaned at the same time.

Maddie leaned away from them. "What did I do?"

Rachel said, "I already tried to match her up with him."

Maddie laughed and glanced over to where Andy stood, talking to two of his brothers. "It just that he's so kind. He deserves someone like that."

"Thank you. But I'm here for a short time. Then Gracie and I have lives to get back to in Anchorage."

Sam noticed Mrs. O'Connell walking toward them.

Rachel whispered, "I don't think she believes that you're just a client."

The older woman stopped and smiled at them. "If this is the girls' conversation, can I join?"

Sam almost said, *as long as you don't try to match me up with your son*, but she caught herself in time. That might not go over as well with his mother.

Rachel stood in a hurry to get a fourth chair and pulled it over to their group. "You're always welcome to join us, Mrs. O'Connell."

"Mom. Or Anita, at the very least."

Rachel nodded. "I'm trying. I think I called you the right thing last time we were down."

Mrs. O'Connell turned to Sam with a big grin on her face. "You and Andy are great together in the kitchen."

Rachel covered her mouth with her hand, but Sam heard her snicker.

"Andy is an excellent cook."

His mother frowned. "That is true, but—"

Rachel said, "The lasagna was delicious, wasn't it?"

Sam jumped in at Rachel's lead. "Thank you! I had to make do with everything that Andy had on hand. We didn't have time to go to the store."

As soon as she used the word *we*, Mrs. O'Connell's eyebrows shot up.

"With my vehicle in the shop, I would have had to drive with him if I wanted to go to the grocery store."

Disappointment showed on Mrs. O'Connell's face. At that minute, Lucy meandered by. She bumped Mrs. O'Connell's ankle. Not to be outdone, Kitty was close on her heels. Mrs. O'Connell sat on the chair next to Sam and started petting them.

Samantha looked at Rachel, knowing she had relief clearly written on her face. There had been a successful distraction in the form of four-legged and furry friends.

"I've been trying some new pet treats for cats. Those two have been some of my test subjects."

"I know cats can be finicky, so congratulations if they ate any of them." Andy's mother changed the conversation's direction. "Has your business been going well, Rachel?"

"Great." Rachel fingered the vest she had on over a long-sleeved blouse. "This is one of my newest designs. And I'm going on a spring buying trip soon in the Lower Forty-eight."

"Is Noah going with you?"

"He needs to work because he took time off for our wedding, and he's saving up leave for our delayed honeymoon."

Mrs. O'Connell's eyes lit up at the words *wedding* and *honeymoon*. "You had a beautiful wedding, my dear." When she turned her attention toward Sam, she hoped it was with a light inquiry, something simple about her life that she would be happy to discuss.

"Are you single, Samantha?"

Nope. Not a simple answer.

"Yes, ma'am. But I'm busy with my business right now. Too busy for any sort of relationship beyond one between me and my dog." Gracie chose that moment to appear at her side.

Mrs. O'Connell wore a very serious expression. "When you share your life with someone, it makes your load lighter, you know."

How could she get away from here gracefully? She did not want to hurt this woman's feelings, but she was definitely pushing her toward a son who had shown zero interest. And she was not interested in him, anyway. Right? *Note to self, become more convinced of your decisions.*

Rachel gave a small shrug to indicate that she didn't know what to do.

When Sam turned toward Maddie, she could see a decision being made. She hoped Maddie could help. At least the other woman didn't shrug or shake her head.

Maddie leaned over toward Sam. "There are any number of things that can distract her temporarily, but she'll be back on you within minutes. However, there's one thing that will distract her for a long time."

Sam was about to ask what that was and if she had the power to invoke it, when Maddie stood and looked around the room, her gaze stopping on her husband. He turned in her direction at that moment, and she gave a slight nod. He looked hesitantly around the room, and then he walked toward her, his smile growing wider with each step.

When he arrived, she said, "I think it's time now. Is that okay with you?"

Mrs. O'Connell said, "For what? Are you leaving so soon? I hope not."

Mark clapped his hands. "Everyone!" The room grew silent as they all focused on him. He put his arm around Maddie and pulled her to his side. "We were going to wait to share this news, but we're going to tell you now. We're expecting a baby in about six months."

Mrs. O'Connell gasped and covered her mouth with her hand. She swallowed hard. "Is this true?"

"Mom, this is not something I would tease you about. I promise."

The grandmother-to-be's lip quivered. "I'm so happy." She rose to her feet and hurried over to hug her son and daughter-in-law.

More hugs were exchanged.

Rachel and Sam watched the family interact. When the moment passed, Rachel turned toward Sam and said in a low voice, "Maddie is right. Mrs. O'Connell has wanted grand-children for a very long time. She asked me once if I was expecting when I'd gained a few pounds over the holidays. I hurriedly lost that weight."

Sam grinned.

"It isn't that we don't want children. But we're definitely waiting until we've been married longer." She stood and went over to give her sister- and brother-in-law hugs.

"Have you chosen names yet?"

"Do you know if it's a boy or girl?"

Sam watched as questions flew around the room, Maddie answering them as quickly as they were fired at her.

Maddie laughed. "Everyone!"

The room became quiet.

"It's too soon to know the baby's sex."

Murmurs went around the room.

"And we haven't decided if we want to know, anyway."

"You're naming him for me, aren't you?" the proud grandpa-to-be asked, but with a tongue-in-cheek expression.

Mark laughed. "We haven't made a list of names yet." Then he looked at his wife and said, "I'm going to be a father." The sense of wonder in his voice took Sam's breath away.

Everyone except Sam crowded around the couple for a hug. Gracie came over to Sam and leaned against her legs, probably because the exuberance of the humans had overwhelmed her.

Sam rubbed the dog's side. "It's okay, Gracie. Everyone is happy."

Andy walked over to her and plopped down in one of the chairs. "I'm going to be an uncle."

She laughed. "You are. Will you be a doting uncle who spoils your niece or nephew at every opportunity you get?"

He grinned. "I probably will."

Something about this man told her that not only would he be an amazing uncle, but that he would be a wonderful father. "It looks as though your mother has been thoroughly distracted from the subject of me being your houseguest."

He watched his mother for a moment before replying. "She has been. For now. Only time will tell if it's going to be permanent."

Sam leaned forward. "This might be a good time to serve dessert. If only I could write something about the baby on the cake. I've had to help with pastry decorating a time or two, and the results aren't always pretty."

"I know it sounds strange, but I can do it. Last winter, I got bored and watched a bunch of videos on cake decorating. I didn't reach the sophisticated levels of roses or anything like that, but I can write on a cake pretty well. My room-mates weren't impressed, though."

She stared at him for moment, trying to figure out who he meant, then chuckled. "You didn't wow the cats?"

His shoulders slumped. "No. They weren't excited about my new skills." Then he looked up and grinned.

Sam chuckled, then said, "I know the humans will appreciate it." In the kitchen, she whipped up a small batch of white frosting and split it into two bowls. Andy added food coloring to each to make a soft baby blue and pink. Then he filled cake decorating bags and wrote *Mommy & Daddy to be* on the cake, varying pink and blue for each word.

And her heart melted.

Holding a knife in her hands, Sam said, "I had planned to cut squares of cake and put them on plates, but everyone needs to see this first."

He clapped his hands loudly. "Okay everyone, come see the dessert so we can cut it up and serve it." They crowded around it and there were *oohs* and *ahhs*.

Rachel said, "Nice job on the cake decorating, Sam."

Sam laughed. "Don't look at me. When I say that I am not a pastry chef, I mean it."

Rachel had a puzzled expression. "But what about the cake?"

"Great-Great Aunt Gertie's recipe. I can follow directions, but don't expect any spun sugar or cake sculpting. I can promise, though, that it's delicious. *Andy* wrote on it."

Sam started cutting and serving the cake. Each person accepted their piece with a smile. This did seem to be a nice family. They couldn't have been happier about the coming baby. Of course, her family would be that same way, but they were spread out across the globe and didn't get together very often. Two of her sisters weren't even on this continent. The day wrapped up with joy about the baby pushing away all questions about her and Andy. Sam covered the leftover cake as the visitors donned their coats and prepared to leave.

Andy stepped over next to her.

"I think we're in the clear," she whispered.

Out of the corner of her eye, Sam noticed that his mother and father looked at each other and gave a nod. She hoped that didn't mean that there was approval for the two of them being a good couple. Not that she'd think that was a bad thing. But this wasn't your ordinary nod.

Andy watched everyone and didn't say anything. Sam glanced up at him, but he seemed focused on the scene in front of them. Once his parents had their boots on and his mom had pulled her knit hat on her head and slipped her gloves on, Sam was feeling pretty good about the situation. But Andy still hadn't said a word, and he knew these people a lot better than she did.

CHAPTER FIFTEEN

*H*is mother came toward them. "I've given this a lot of thought. You know how I feel about unmarried couples being alone together. I know Rachel and Noah were lost together in the wilderness for days with no one but a big furry dog between them. I believe that what they say happened is what happened. But I didn't have any control over that situation. I do have control over this one. I'm going to go home and get some things. I'll be back in a few hours so you're not here alone together." She smiled at them.

The words Andy had uttered earlier came back to haunt him. That was his worst mistake, maybe ever, and was creating the nightmare that was beginning. He had not shared a home with his mother for a long time. He had his routine, and that was how he got his work done. Sam had been easy to live with, but his mother wouldn't bend to his schedule; she would want to set hers.

Noah hurried over. "Rachel's going out of state for her

buying trip, so I can stay here. You won't need to take time out of your schedule, Mom."

Before he caught himself, Andy said, "But don't you have to fly for work, Noah?" As soon as he'd spoken, he thought, *You idiot. Your brother's offering to help you out.* He must have figured out the logistics of it before he'd done that.

His mother said, "He's right, Noah. You shouldn't have to lose flight time when I just need to rearrange some volunteer activities and delay chores with some of our rental properties."

Andy noticed Jack talking to Aimee in a hush-hush way, then Jack hurried over. "Actually, I think it would be easiest if I took care of this. Aimee is in the middle of another one of her big jewelry-making projects. She works from her home studio now, so I don't need to help her. And I certainly don't have anything to take pictures of right now. Besides, I'll be here for sunrise over a frozen lake. And I know I saw snow-shoe hare footprints behind the house when I went out to check on the dogs."

Andy didn't have to force enthusiasm into his reply. "That's a great idea, Jack! You don't have to take any time off work. Aimee's busy anyway, and you can get some great pictures."

Andy hugged his mother. "That was a very generous offer, Mom. I'm glad that you didn't have to do that, though. With his current situation, Jack is the most obvious choice in the family." He held his breath, waiting for her reply.

His mother looked from one brother to the other and then to Sam. Her level of suspicion had not lessened, but she knew when to step back. "I respect both Sam and Andy, but I want to make sure everything's okay. Jack, you watch these two. It's on you."

"Yes, ma'am. I'll make sure nothing untoward happens."

When everyone had cleared out of the house except for Jack and Aimee, the breath Andy had been holding whooshed out of him. He leaned against the kitchen counter. "Wow."

Jack said, "I can't even imagine what it would be like if Mom took over your house."

Sam said, "Took over your house? Isn't that extreme? Wouldn't she spend time in her room, maybe read or watch a little TV?"

Everyone looked at her like she'd lost her mind.

"I dearly love that woman," Aimee said. "But her idea of being useful is to do as much as she possibly can. That's an excellent quality in a person. Her house is organized."

Jack picked up the conversation. "She would have taken everything out of the kitchen cupboards and reorganized it. To help. She would have cleaned every inch of the house. Of course she would make sure that both of you were able to fully participate in anything she was doing. She enjoys having her family around her. I wouldn't be surprised if you had some new shelving units installed in your basement before you were done."

When Jack chuckled, everyone except Sam joined in.

She bit her lip and her eyes were bright, so she was trying to hold in laughter. Grinning, she said, "Then I wholeheart- edly thank you, Jack, for agreeing to do this. But we don't really need to have you stay, do we, Andy? We were doing fine on the no hanky-panky before she arrived." She giggled after she said the words *hanky-panky*.

Andy gasped. "You don't get it, do you? As long as you're here, you're open to spot checks. She will call to check every day. She'll probably ask for each of us to weigh in on some situation so she can check to make sure everything is as it should be."

Sam's expression changed from a smile to a frown.

"Sam, she's a wonderful, bighearted woman. She loves her family and wants to make sure nothing happens to hurt anyone."

"Okay." She drew the word out slowly. "I think I need to thank you, Jack."

Andy patted his brother on the shoulder. "It's going to be a long day for you. The good news, though, is that you get not only my cooking but also Sam's while you're here."

Jack's expression brightened. "I hadn't thought of that. I won't have a plain sandwich for lunch, will I?" He looked right at Sam when he said that.

"What do you like?"

Andy and Aimee laughed.

"Jack loves food," Aimee said. "He's just a terrible cook, so maybe you can give him some pointers when he's here. We're getting married this fall, and I don't know how to cook either. It's going to be microwave dinners for us."

Both Sam and Andy shuddered.

"Hey, don't knock them. There's really good stuff out there."

Sam raised an eyebrow, and Andy grinned.

"Andy will be working, so I'm on lunch duty. We can have leftovers from today. I'll have to get back to you about dinner tomorrow night."

"Lunch was so good that I'm sure that will be too."

Sam asked, "Jack, can we give you a grocery list? There must be stores in Homer."

"There are. We're going to be on our way. Have Andy text me your list. Be very specific. Remember that a non-cook will be shopping for you." Jack and Aimee started for the door.

Sam grinned. "I'll keep that in mind."

When it was finally the two of them and their pets, Andy sat on the living room couch. Sam followed him and chose the chair across from him.

He reached out and absently petted the cat that jumped up beside him, Lucy. "Thank you, Sam, for putting up with all of my family's shenanigans."

She leaned back in her chair. "I won't say it wasn't stressful at times. But I do need to say that they are a nice bunch of people, your family. It must be wonderful to see them this often."

Sometimes he forgot to be grateful for the fact that his family *now* all lived fairly close together. Mark and Noah had been in the military. Jack had spent years up north in Fairbanks, much too far to come for lunch. Adam spent years going to school Outside, but found a teaching position in Anchorage afterward.

"Until the last few years, not very many of us lived near here. And then, one by one, we either returned to Alaska or moved closer within Alaska. Now I think the one with the longest drive is Mark, followed by Adam. They're actually fairly close together beyond Anchorage in Birchwood and Palmer."

Sam nodded, probably because she knew where those places were.

"Jack's in Homer and Noah's now in Anchorage." He rubbed his hand over his face. "I'm going to church in the morning. You're welcome to come—if you want to."

She nodded. "I'd like that."

"I'll need to leave about nine." He pushed to his feet. "Let's get this kitchen cleaned up, and I'll get back to work. I gave Jack a key, so he can let himself in whenever he arrives."

"I'll take care of the kitchen."

"If you're sure?" She gave a single nod and Andy went off toward his office.

The next morning, Sam stared down at the cats who were watching her. "I'm sorry, girls, but Andy is still asleep. Jack must be too, but he probably doesn't know how to feed you anyway."

They sat down and continued to watch her. It felt like a lion pride eyeing its prey. When the orange cat walked over to her, she clenched up. Lucy had jumped on her lap once in her fit of jealousy and Kitty had slept on the bed next to Gracie, but otherwise, the cats, while pleasant, had kept their distance. Lucy bumped against her leg, sat down again, and mewed.

"Perhaps I overreacted about all of you. You're nice, aren't you?"

A mew went up from the gray-and-white cat—Kitty.

"I need to ask him what to feed you, since I'm up earlier and you seem to be ready to eat."

She fed Gracie, glad that Jack had found their usual brand at the store in Homer.

Sam decided a little fresh salmon with no seasoning on it couldn't hurt the cats. At least she hoped not. She'd set some aside yesterday to test more treats with. When she opened up the container, the cats went wild.

"Cats and fish. That's a natural, right?"

The four felines twined themselves around her legs. Sam

put a pinch of salmon onto plates and set one in front of each of them.

She looked up for a few seconds and then back down at what were now licked-clean plates. The orange cat meowed loudly, so she got out the treats Andy had approved of and put one on each of the plates. The cats dove in and gobbled them up. Those treats had been a one hundred percent fail with Gracie, but at least the cats were enjoying them.

"So what are we going to do today?"

Her dog stepped closer to her and the cats backed away. When Gracie sniffed Lucy, Sam said, "No, Gracie!" The cat reached out its paw and popped Gracie on the nose.

Sam crouched down to look at her pet's nose, and she found no scratches. The cat had fired a warning shot. She knelt closer and kissed Gracie on the nose. "You have to be careful around them. They aren't other dogs." And then she realized that two of the cats hadn't backed away. She petted Happy who purred . . . happily. She reached toward Kitty who pushed into her hand and started purring as Sam petted her. "I think I'm starting to understand the love of cats."

Once Gracie had eaten, Sam herded her back to their side of the house so she could more or less keep an eye on her while she got ready. After checking on Petunia and her kittens, her dog curled up on the bed, and Sam went in to take a shower and get ready for church. When she came out to the great room, she found Andy with wet hair and the nicest outfit she'd seen on him so far. It was still a flannel shirt, but fairly new and this time paired with nice cords. This was dressed-up for Alaska. "Good morning!"

Andy set three bowls of food onto the kitchen counter and the cats jumped up to eat. "It's actually a good morning. I had planned to stay up late and work, but that whole thing with my family yesterday seemed to wear me out. I decided to relax for a while and read a book, but fell asleep with it open beside me."

He took a bowl down the hall to Petunia. When he returned, he said, "I've heard people talk about morning. They said it was bright out, and that it was like the start of a whole new day."

"Is it everything you'd heard it was?" Grinning, she sat at one of the barstools at the island.

"It's different. Don't get me wrong, I'm glad I got a good night's sleep before church so I'm not struggling to listen, but it would have been nice to finish that client's website."

She'd taken too much of his time.

"Don't get that guilty expression again, Sam. This isn't because I've been working on your site; this is because they keep adding to theirs. I must have started this thing in August last year. It's for a major corporation, though, and they keep paying the bills I submit to them, so it's not a bad situation. But I can't even begin to tell you how much I'm looking forward to having this completed."

"So, when are we leaving for church?"

"First, I'm happy to have you join me. It's a small church with friendly people, and you will definitely be welcomed. Just realize that you will experience a situation similar to being with my family. A small church becomes extended family."

Sam waved that thought away. "If I can survive lunch with your real family, I think I'll be fine. Am I dressed okay?"

Andy looked at her from top to bottom, then back up. "You look great. Don't get me wrong, but isn't that what you wore yesterday? I'm a guy and guys don't always notice those things, but I think you did." He turned red as he discussed his observation of her clothing.

"Andy, I had a sum total of two outfits when I arrived. Petunia had her kittens on one outfit. And this is the other one."

"I am so sorry, Sam! I didn't realize that she'd ruined fifty percent of your wardrobe. We can stop and pick something else up. Although I'm not sure what's going to be open on a Sunday this far from the city."

"It's okay. I talked to Rachel yesterday. She's going to my apartment today and will overnight me a bunch of stuff. If I wash this and have it clean each day until then, I'll be okay."

"I think we're probably a similar size, if you want to wear any of my shirts."

Wearing a man's clothing seemed very intimate. *Remember Sam, this has nothing to do with any feelings he has toward you. He's just a nice guy.* "I'll be fine. But thank you for your offer. By the way, your cats were very hungry, so I gave them each one of the salmon dog treats. Maybe you should give me the full instructions for feeding them so I can take care of it in the morning. Because odds are you aren't going to sleep early tonight."

He grinned. "You're probably right about that." Andy took some cans of cat food out of a cupboard and explained how much to put in each of the bowls. "Did they all enjoy the treat?"

Sam laughed. "I wish I could tell you that I watched them savor every morsel, but I looked down and the treats were gone."

Andy laughed. "I would take that as an affirmative on the feline enjoyment factor." He checked his watch. "We need to leave in about a half hour."

Jack walked into the room, yawning. Rubbing his eyes, he said, "After I take a shower, I'm going to head to Homer to spend the day with Aimee."

Sam asked, "Will you be home for lunch?"

"Aimee and I talked about it on the way home yesterday. No to lunch, but definitely yes to dinner. Speaking of lunch, though, you wouldn't have any of that delicious lasagna left, would you?" He raised an eyebrow. "I'd love to take enough to Aimee for us to eat."

She'd cooking professionally for years, but it still made her happy when someone loved her food. "I do. I'll pack it for you. If I don't see you again before we go, I'll leave it on the kitchen counter."

"Thanks!" Jack hurried back down the hall.

She packed up the leftovers and put them where she'd said she would, then they left.

When they walked into the small church, Sam wondered if she'd made a mistake. All eyes were on them, and she continued feeling that as the service began. She perched on the pew and didn't hear a word said during the service.

When it ended, several people came up to them, and Andy introduced her as a visiting client. She wasn't sure they believed him, though, because more than one person said they looked forward to seeing her in the future.

On the drive home, she said, "Whew! I'm not sure they believed I'm a client."

Andy drove for a while without responding. "Maybe we didn't look like business associates to them."

She wondered about that too.

～

When they were home, Sam sat down at the kitchen island with her computer and went to work on dog treat ideas. Andy played with his cats, something he said he enjoyed taking time to do on Sunday afternoons. She'd gone through the ingredient lists for high-end dog foods to see what they had found dogs liked. That didn't always work for her treats, but it gave her a good starting point.

She'd keep the salmon one on the back burner since Gracie would eat salmon but didn't like that treat. It would be a very Alaskan treat and customers might like that—if she found a combination of ingredients her dog liked. Turkey appeared to be a likely next candidate. Without looking up, she said, "Andy, do you have any turkey in the freezer?"

"Actually I have two turkey breasts in the freezer. I had bought them thinking they'd be a nice change from a whole turkey for Thanksgiving."

"Your mom didn't like breaking tradition, did she?"

"Not a bit. I keep meaning to get out one of those turkey breasts and roast it for dinner. Are we going to have Thanksgiving in March?"

She looked up from her keyboard. "I'm actually working on dog treat ideas. I wanted to do a test run of some turkey ones with Gracie."

Lucy meowed.

"That sounded more like an 'I'd love to have a turkey treat' meow to me. Wasn't it, Lucy?" He crouched to pet the cat.

Sam grinned. "Would she, now? You'll have to let her know Goodness Gracie! only makes dog treats."

Andy washed out the bowl and set it on the counter. "Why is that, Sam?"

She looked up at him with a furrowed brow. "Why is what?"

"Why does Goodness Gracie! only make dog treats?"

"Um, because I own a dog. I started out making treats for her and that turned into a business. Besides, dogs are man's best friend."

"The numbers show that cats may be America's favorite pet."

"Oh, don't get me started on this cat-versus-dog thing." She chuckled and sat back in her seat. "I'm sure we could go on about that all day."

"Either way, that means that there are a lot of customers for cat treats."

"But I don't know how to make treats for cats."

"You already did."

She realized he was right. "I did, didn't I? I'd have to do more research, of course, to see what cats like and should or shouldn't eat. And then I'd have to do a bunch of test samples and have cats show me if they like them or not."

He gestured at his cluster of cats. "Would you guys like to test new cat treats? Maybe help Sam out so she can decide what cats like?"

A loud meow sounded from one of them.

Both Andy and Sam laughed.

"Well, I seem to have extra time right now. When I get my business back up and running—"

"Which will be later today. I promise."

Sam gave a single nod. "I hope it's in time. My revenue is way down."

"But if you had more buyers for treats, wouldn't that help? Maybe you could have people preorder the flavors the cats enjoy, and you can manufacture them when you get back to your commercial kitchen."

Sam stood and hugged him, enjoying it far too much. "That's genius, Andy! I accept the challenge." She hurried around the island and into the kitchen. "I want to test some new treats today."

"Let's get started on them."

She cocked her head to the side and looked at him. "Don't you have a website to work on, mister?"

"I almost always have a website to work on. Lately, I've had several at one time I could be working on. I think I'd like to take a break and do this."

"What about the website you're working on for that entrepreneur?" At his questioning expression, she added, "The owner of the pet treat company."

He laughed. "Her website will only take about two hours to finish. More or less." He waved his hand from side to side. "The others are ongoing projects. No matter how much I did today, I'd still have more tomorrow."

"I love diving into a project."

"You didn't begin working on the dinner for my family right away."

She rolled her eyes. "Andy, remember that was *easy*. If you'd asked me to make a meal for two hundred, then I would have done some prep work."

"By the way, I noticed you now said you had a *pet treat* company. Not a dog treat company."

Sam thought back over her words. "I did, didn't I? If I've gotten used to it that quickly, this must be a good plan, right?"

"Must be. What kind of treat do you want to make first? What did your research say?"

"I don't want to sound offensive to a cat lover, but I got the distinct impression cats were a bit finicky."

Andy grinned. "There isn't a cat lover on earth who would take offense at that statement. I once heard it said that it was good to have a dog and a cat because the dog would be the vacuum cleaner for anything the cat wouldn't eat. And there tend to be a fair number of those things."

Sam chewed her lip. "Are you sure this is a good idea?"

He picked up Lucy and held her in his arms. "This is a cat who will eat anything with fish in it. *Anything.* If I open up a can of tuna for a salad, she's right there. Salmon for dinner? Oh, yeah. I know that, so I will buy a treat with fish." He pointed toward Kitty. "She loves fish too. But her weakness is pumpkin. She loves it. Oh, and cheese. I guess some cats have problems with cheese. They're lactose intolerant. Not Kitty. Adores it. So I would buy a cheesy pumpkin treat."

"So what you're telling me is that cats are picky, but they're consistently picky."

"Yes and no. But starting with two kinds of treats would be a good way to go. I wouldn't begin with one. I have more salmon in the freezer if you want to start with that. We could thaw it out quickly in the microwave."

"That sounds like a plan. With someone else I would have to ask, do you have a food grinder? But with you, I know you must have one even though I didn't notice it. It could have been in the pantry, but I was spellbound by my many options." She started in that direction.

Andy put his hand on her shoulder. Sam felt the tingle and spark go through her whole body and struggled to keep a normal expression on her face. She wanted to lean against his hand to feel more sparks.

Andy left his hand there for a few seconds, then jerked it

away. Maybe he wasn't unaffected. Clearing his throat, he seemed to have trouble focusing. Then he said, "I have a grinding attachment that goes on to the mixer. I use it so rarely that it's actually in a box in the garage. I can go get that." He started toward the garage door.

If he'd dismissed what had happened, she needed to too. *Focus, Sam.* "Please pull some salmon out of the freezer too. The problem is that it's going to make the treats expensive if I have to use fresh salmon."

"You're planning to test a turkey treat for Gracie. Why don't we make the second cat treat turkey, and you can put some pumpkin into it?"

"You must have pumpkin or you wouldn't be saying that."

"I know I have a few cans on the shelf because of Kitty's love of it. Every once in a while, I put a spoonful in her food. It also helps kitties if they aren't pooping as often as they should be." When Sam winced, he said, "Too much information?"

"Yes and no. If I'm going to sell it to cats, I should know what pumpkin can do to them. So we go light on the pumpkin."

"That's probably best."

"Grab a package of blueberries from the freezer too. I seem to remember seeing them on the good-for-cats list."

"Will do." He returned with his arms full. "You can thaw the meat in the microwave. Or maybe you have a chef trick. I'll go back to work. Let me know when we can get started and I'll stop my work. I might be able to get your website finished before then."

Sam grinned. "That's the best news I've heard all day. Speaking of food, what do you want for lunch?"

Andy had already started walking away. Without turning

around he said, "Surprise me. I seriously doubt there's anything you could make that I wouldn't want to eat." He disappeared through his office door, and she heard it click shut.

Sam turned toward the pets. "Okay, guys. Let's do more research on treats." She put the salmon and turkey in containers large enough to hold them and cold water. With a timer set for an hour, she opened a document on her computer, the place where she would make notes of ingredients used, proportions, and recipe ideas. When the alarm went off, she checked the meat. The salmon had thawed, but the thicker turkey needed more time.

Thinking ahead, she decided to slow cook stew for dinner. She cut the rest of the roast they'd used for the stir-fry into chunks, browned it, and put carrots, potatoes, onions, and more in a pot at a low simmer on the back of the stove. It would be ready whenever they were.

At lunchtime, Sam got out the last of the lasagna, then she realized they needed something to go with it. Yesterday, she'd had the roasted vegetables, but they'd all been eaten. Thanks to Jack's shopping, they now had lettuce. She put some in each of two bowls and went through the pantry to see what Andy had to add to it. Once she'd topped the lettuce with dried blueberries from a glass jar that said his mother had dried them last year, sunflower seeds, chopped pecans, and Parmesan cheese she grated from a block in the fridge, she thought she had a tasty salad for them. After whipping up a balsamic vinaigrette, she was set.

~

Sam knocked on his office door, then loudly said, "I fixed lunch *and* we're ready to roll on the treats."

He opened the door and rubbed his hands together with glee. "This should be fun. I'm not used to having anybody to cook with."

"Ever?"

"My longest relationship was with someone who didn't really get too excited about food. She ate, but she definitely was not a foodie." Andy thought it over. "No. I don't think I've ever had anyone to cook with other than Mom when I was growing up. I'm glad you're here, Sam." As soon as he said those words, he regretted them. He didn't want to lead her on. She was here for a short time, and he was certainly not in any way ready to date. He wasn't sure he ever would be.

They ate side by side at the kitchen island, and he could feel her nearness. He liked it but didn't want to get used to it. When he took a bite of his salad, the flavors popped on his tongue. "This is great! What did you do here?"

"I threw in some things I found in your pantry."

"I guess it's the perspective of a trained chef that does it. The combination is delicious. And this dressing? Wow!"

"It makes me happy when someone enjoys the food I made."

He took another bite and savored it. "Sam, I could weigh fifty pounds more in the week you're here."

"No, I'm keeping it fairly healthy. There's really nothing about that salad that's anything but healthy. Now, the lasagna is somewhat higher in the guilt factor, but it's leftovers. Besides, now that Jack's going to be here every night, we can spread the calories between three people instead of two. If I make dessert, you won't get to hog it all."

Andy laughed. "That is truer than you realize. That boy can eat. But I guess he burns it off in his work now that he's doing the outdoor photography. He goes on some long treks and spends hours out in the winter cold."

As soon as they'd finished, Sam grabbed the dishes, rinsed them off, and put them in the dishwasher. "Now, are you ready to help me with these cat treats?"

She had an uncertainty to her voice that she didn't have when it came to the dog treats—or the human food, for that matter.

"Sam, this isn't going to be hard. Don't worry, and remember they already love the salmon one you made for Gracie."

She put her shoulders back and more confidently said, "That's true. Okay, let's do this."

As they started working, he could still feel her nervousness and it cast a blanket over them. He needed to liven up the scene. "Let me put some music on. Something with a lively beat to make cat food by."

She smiled. "You have an album that's titled Cat Treat Sonata or Cooking for Kitty?"

He could feel her loosening up already. "I was thinking maybe something with a Latin beat. Kind of soft, not salsa, but fun."

"Works for me."

Andy did as he'd said, and music soon filled the room. He soon noticed Sam relaxing as she sliced and diced.

~

As she stood beside Andy, he swayed to the music. She bumped her hip against his. He looked up at her with surprise in his eyes, but he bumped her back.

Then noise from the meat grinder drowned out the sound of the music. When he turned it off, a lively rhythm played. An oldie.

Sam said, "Ooh! A rumba. I love that dance."

Andy cocked an eyebrow at her. "You know how to dance?"

"Don't tell me that you can build websites at some kind of genius level, you're an amazing cook, and you do Latin ballroom dancing? I didn't think there was a person like that on earth."

"Mom decided we should know how to do ballroom dancing in case we were ever at an event and it was required of us. Again, I'm the youngest—"

"I get it. So she had more years to do that with you after she had the idea."

"Yep."

"Don't tell me she had you compete in dancing?"

His face turned red. "She tried. Dad put his foot down there. We all enjoyed the outdoors and grew up on the water in small-town Alaska. That suited Dad. His teenage son doing ballroom dancing competitions crossed some major boundaries for him."

She eyed him. "Would you have wanted to?"

"I'm fairly competitive. I knew how to do the dance. And I've got moves." He said those last words with a swing of his hips.

"I am not a dancing genius."

He looked defeated.

"But I do know how to do a few of them and the rumba is

one of those." She held her hands up in the correct position. "Show me what you've got."

Before she knew it, Andy had danced them out of the kitchen and into the center of the living area. Gracie had been lying next to one of the cats, Happy this time, so her friends list was growing. She looked up at the movement and watched them as they passed by. Andy swung Sam to the side and back, then did a dip as the song closed.

He looked in her eyes for a moment, and she was sure he would kiss her any second. Warmth rushed through her as she waited. But he brought her upright and stepped back, putting his hands behind him as though to avoid temptation.

Interesting. Maybe another dance would help the situation. "That was great! Do you have any waltz moves? That's actually my favorite."

He grinned. "I do." He searched on his phone and found a Viennese waltz. Soon, Latin America was replaced by Austria. He held up his hands this time, and she went into his arms. She had to count in her head—*one two three, one two three*—for a while until she got the feel of it again. Then she was able to let go and let him lead her around the room. As she swirled in his arms, she could imagine herself in an old-fashioned ball gown with Andy dressed up in a waistcoat and breeches. When the song ended, he stepped back and did a formal bow. "Thank you, milady."

She felt cheated when there wasn't an almost-kiss this time. "I could see us back in time."

"Me too."

She was facing the kitchen. "I don't think they had cat treats then."

"They've always had cat treats. But no one went to all this effort for them. I have four spoiled little beasts."

"Four very happy, spoiled little beasts with four more tiny new ones."

Andy grinned. "True."

They spent another hour mixing up the treats, and then Sam rolled out some of each flavor and cut them into small pieces so they could bake. When she could smell them cooking, three cats lined up at the entrance to the kitchen.

She pointed over at them. "Look, Andy."

He laughed. "We know they passed the smell test."

Gracie came over behind the cats.

"And the dog too. We may have something here after all."

When the treats came out of the oven, Sam set the pans outside on the front step again so they could cool quickly. She cleaned the kitchen as they waited, and Andy went to his office to send an email to a client.

A couple of minutes after she brought the treats inside, Jack opened the door, and Andy came out to greet him.

Jack sniffed the air. "Yum! Is that dinner? Or did I miss whatever this wonderful smell was at lunch?" He started to unzip his coat.

Andy laughed. "Lunch has long since passed. What you smell is cat and dog treats. But you can have one. If the cats and Gracie decide you're worthy."

Jack grimaced and looked down at the pets. "Thank you, ladies, but I think I will let you keep those to yourself. At least tell me that there's going to be something good for dinner."

"Contrary to what your brother led you to believe, if you smell something like beef stew, that actually is your nose working correctly," Sam said. "I've got it on a low temperature on the stove. That's our dinner."

He did a fist pump. "I always eat well when I'm around Andy. The two of you together are quite a team."

For a second, Andy stared at his brother and frowned. Was he wondering if Jack been matchmaking? She didn't think he had been.

"Are you ready to give the treats a try?" Sam looked at Andy.

He let out a big sigh. His brothers' matchmaking upset him more than she'd expect it to. Then he focused on the treats. "Let's do it."

Sam set one of each treat in front of each of the cats and called Gracie over to get her own turkey treat so she wouldn't gobble anyone's up or scare the kitties. Gracie sniffed her treat, licked it, then ate it in one bite.

"Score on the turkey dog treat." Sam rubbed Gracie on the head. "Good girl. You make the best taste tester ever. Thank you."

Gracie sat down and wagged her tail happily.

Sam checked the cats. "How did we do there?"

"They all ate the salmon treat. And two of them ate the turkey one. No, wait. Kitty scarfed it down. We are three for three on the treats. We should take one to Petunia to see what new mothers think."

Jack looked between the two of them. "I've apparently missed something. Don't you do dog treats, Sam?"

"I did. I made some dog treats that the cats loved but Gracie wouldn't touch. Andy suggested I broaden my business. It's a good plan, especially since right now I have four feline taste testers. I'll need to get these taken care of and nailed down before my SUV is ready and I go home." Leaving didn't sound as appealing as it had before.

A while later, Sam packed the treats in storage containers and left them sealed on the counter. By then it was time for dinner. She got out a bowl to make some biscuits for the humans. Her skills might not extend to fine pastry, but her mother hadn't let any of them leave home without being able to make a decent biscuit. In fact, that was the one food her oldest sister could make. Ella once said that when she first got out of college, she didn't have much money, but fortunately the ingredients for biscuits were cheap. Sam slid those in the oven and watched as Andy and his brother went over to the living room and sat down to chat.

Andy stopped talking to Jack and said, "Sam, you don't need me to help, do you?"

"Of course not. But thank you for asking. In about ten minutes, maybe you could get some drinks for all of us."

He nodded. And then he and Jack started talking about a website. Apparently Andy had been encouraging Jack to have a website to sell his work for a very long time and had finally started working on it in spare moments. He didn't seem to have too many of those lately.

CHAPTER SIXTEEN

*A*ndy watched Sam out the window. She threw a stick, probably one from his woodpile, and Gracie pranced back to her with it. The dog proudly dropped it at her feet and sat waiting for another round of fetch.

Sam embraced every moment of every day with an energy that invigorated him and made him smile. He would have thought it would wear him out, but it didn't because she had a calm attitude while she buzzed with activity. That must be because of years in a chaotic restaurant kitchen. Or maybe she was naturally that way, and that's why she'd done well in that setting.

Yesterday, when she'd mentioned testing cat treats before she went home, Andy had felt like he had been punched in his stomach. Sam would leave. Of course she would. He knew that in his head, but his heart had just gotten the message. It wasn't the same as when Lori left him. Maybe this is what it felt like when you made a friend in a short amount of time and you got used to them being nearby. Yes, that was it.

The dog brought back the stick again. Sam laughed as she threw it, and Gracie chased after it.

Jack spoke from his side and startled him. He hadn't even realized that his brother was there.

"I'd ask what you're looking at, but that's obvious. She's something, isn't she?"

Andy chuckled. "She is that." He watched her throw the stick again, and Gracie joyfully ran back with it. "I stepped away from my computer to see what was happening with everybody and it was quiet, so I looked out the window."

"I was in my room working on some photos. I cleaned up a few and submitted them to different sites to sell. But I think you may be having more fun."

Andy thought through what his brother had said and stepped backward. He waved both hands in front of himself. "Do not get any ideas about the two of us. She's just my houseguest. Mom called a few minutes ago to check on us."

"I knew she would." They watched out the window for another moment. "Andy, we're guys, so we don't talk much about this stuff, but you know that last year I was helping Aimee in her store. That was it. Only helping."

"What happened?"

Jack turned to face the window. "I still can't tell you. From the first moment I saw her, I thought she was fun and interesting and pretty."

Andy had thought those same things about Sam. Well, at least the second time he saw her. And after she was conscious.

"We became friends. That happened in an oddly quick way. And I didn't want to admit it to myself when we became more than friends. I can't pinpoint the moment it happened."

"So you're saying that Sam and I are more than friends?"

"No! I'm not saying that at all."

"Okay, now I'm confused. What are you telling me, Jack?"

Jack sighed. "I'm not sure what I'm saying. Except that I want you to look beyond the *no* to a *maybe*."

Every time Andy thought about having a relationship, Lori came to mind. "Lori put photos of her new baby up on social media yesterday."

"Are you still friends with her? What are you doing, Andy?"

"Hey, it wasn't me. We have lots of mutual friends. Someone liked it, and there it was."

"Well, as long as we're on all this touchy-feely junk, did it upset you? Or are you over her?"

Andy heard the word *finally* at the end of the last sentence, even if it wasn't spoken. How had he felt? He thought back to that moment. "I thought it was a cute baby. I thought about how the little girl could have been mine."

"But you didn't miss Lori?"

Andy felt like a weight had been lifted. "I didn't miss Lori! That is good news. I am so relieved that's finally happened." He watched Sam for a moment. "Of course, that doesn't mean I want to have a new relationship. Lori hurt me enough that I do not want to repeat it. Not now." Maybe not ever. "Did I ever mention that Lou once told me to stay away from his sister?"

Jack's chuckle surprised him. "She was a kid in his eyes. Is she still a kid?"

Andy watched her for a moment. "Definitely not." He turned and went toward the door. "I know I can have fun with a friend. I'm going to go outside to hang out with Sam and Gracie."

"Throw the stick once for me."

"Hey, come out and throw the stick yourself. You can join the party."

Jack watched him for a moment, and then he said, "No. I think I'm going to go get some more work done. Sometimes I have so much fun taking the photos that I forget I have to do something with them or they won't put a roof over my head."

Andy stopped with one boot half on. "You're okay financially, though, right?"

"I'm doing very well, thank you. It would take me a while to run out of money with the extra that I earned when I sold my business. But I'd really like to keep that in reserve for a long time and live off the proceeds of my photography."

Andy reached for his hat.

"Aimee and I are talking about buying a house of our own sometime in the not-too-distant future."

"I imagine it would get a little tiring to be right there with her grandparents day in and day out."

Jack paused for a second. "I don't really mind having them nearby. They're super nice people and they do a great job of staying out of the way. Now that they successfully helped match us up." He grinned.

Andy pulled on his hat and went out the door, going to the right and around the house to find Sam and Gracie at play. When he was almost there, he stopped and made a snowball. Today's slightly-above-freezing temperatures had turned winter's powdery snow into the perfect snowball ingredient. He peered around the corner, took aim, and threw it at the middle of Sam's back.

She yelped and turned around. Gracie ran toward him with what he'd noticed was her happy bark. Sam gave him a calculating look as she made a snowball of her own. She waved it in the air for a moment as though she was contemplating the best trajectory.

Andy prepared to cover his face or any other part of it in his anatomy the weapon came toward.

She let it fly and hit him right in the middle of his chest.

"Oh. You pack a wallop."

"Girls' softball team three summers running. We took state."

He laughed and brushed the snow off. "Of course you know what this means, don't you?"

She eyed him for a moment. Then, in a sweet voice, she said, "It means you're going to be kind and gentle and not hit me again with a snowball."

He laughed. This woman could make him smile. "It means," he said as he reached down and grabbed a wad of snow in his hands, "that the game is on."

He swung when he was only about halfway upright, catching her off guard. He got her on her lower legs and she went down.

Gracie jumped and danced around her. Sam rolled over laughing. "I'm okay, Gracie. At least I have dry clothes to put on now that the box has come from Rachel."

He held out one hand and helped Sam to her feet. When she stood, they were face to face just inches apart. He looked up at his big window to see if his brother was still there. He was gone, so he'd been honest about going back to work. Andy looked into her brown eyes—her mesmerizing brown eyes.

His heart couldn't break if he kissed her once, could it?

He gently put his hand on the back of her head and Sam looked into his eyes.

Should he do this?

Sam grabbed his collar and pulled him down for a kiss, taking away any options. When his lips touched hers, he wondered how he'd missed this all of his life.

She'd had a week of rash decisions that had gotten her in trouble. When she put her lips on his, she knew this one would get her in the most trouble. And she didn't care. He wrapped his arms around her waist and pulled her close, angling his head so that he could kiss her more deeply. She sighed, and he took that as a request for more, which it was.

Gracie barked three times.

Sam jumped back from Andy and looked around. "That's Gracie's warning bark. She rarely does it." Sam saw a moose in the neighbor's yard heading their way in a hurry. "There!" She pointed. "Gracie, let's go, girl!" She clipped her leash on and tugged on her to get her moving. As they hurried around the corner of the house, Gracie barked three times again.

As they picked up speed, Andy glanced over his shoulder. "Andy! Are we in trouble?"

"I don't know if there's a baby moose around here some-where, but that moose looks like she's on a mission." He picked up Gracie, grabbed Sam's hand, and ran toward the front door.

Inside, Sam leaned against the wall, breathing hard. But not only from the moose. "Andy? What happened?"

He unzipped his coat. "I won't play dumb and ask if you're talking about the moose. But all I can say is, I don't know." He turned to look at her with sad eyes.

"I don't want sadness. Did you enjoy kissing me?"

At that, his face lit up. "More than I should have."

"I'll take that as enough for now."

He looked at her with a questioning expression.

"I don't think I should be kissing anyone."

He shrugged. "I feel the same way. You aren't Lori. You're Sam. But still?"

"Ditto. You aren't Steven. But I'm kinda happy in my life right now. I don't know if I want to mess that up."

Andy hung up his coat and put his boots beside the door. Then he walked away without saying anything else, because what was there to say?

After dinner, Sam went to bed early and stared up at the ceiling in her room with the lamp beside her on. Then she picked up Holly's book. Gracie was now curled up on the bed. An hour later, when she was in the middle of a dramatic scene in the book, Kitty jumped up on the bed. She tentatively moved toward Gracie, then sat down and watched her. Her dog watched the cat but didn't move.

Sam waited to see how this scene would play out. The cat finally inched close enough that she was almost touching her dog, she laid down, and curled up. Gracie closed her eyes again, and the two of them slept. Gracie had made friends with at least two of the cats now, maybe more. Sam turned out the light and closed her eyes.

Tomorrow, she would work on another version of the cat treats. If she was going to try to sell them, she needed to refine her process.

Andy finished her website that afternoon. In spite of what he'd said the day before, they'd had so much fun together that he hadn't done any work on it. They'd had breakfast with Jack, and then his brother had gone south to have lunch with Aimee. It was very sweet that he was willing to drive more than an hour in each direction to eat lunch with his fiancée.

Sam's SUV wasn't ready when she called, but the mechanic said it wouldn't be too much longer. Even though she needed to get back to reality, she didn't know if she wanted to leave here yet.

Each day, Sam perfected the cat treat recipes a little more. The salmon one had been a winner from the beginning. But she tweaked the turkey treat until all four cats gobbled it instantly. That was the one she'd start with. If it didn't go over well, then she'd have to come back and look at the recipe again. At least turkey was inexpensive compared to salmon.

By the end of the week, they'd developed a pattern. Andy spent each day in his office, and she worked on her business. Now that her website was complete and the cat treats were up—an item that could be preordered and delivered in a month—business had soared again. The problem was that she needed to get the dog treats she had in storage delivered to clients, and she was not in Anchorage. On top of that, she was going to need someone to help with her growing business.

CHAPTER SEVENTEEN

$\mathcal{K}$elsey came to mind as the solution. She'd even mentioned her idea to Andy during dinner yesterday. Sam called Kelsey on the chance that she would be willing to help. "How's everything at the restaurant?"

"About the same as when you left. I miss having you here, Sam."

Sam thought about the idea she'd had earlier today. If her friend agreed, it could either go really well or really badly and end her friendship with Kelsey. But it would be her friend's choice to accept or not.

"I know you enjoy cooking, but I also know the hours."

"Sam, I'm just tired. I'm trying to be a good mom, but I feel like I'm always at work. And when I am home, there's so much to do because I'm rarely there."

"You don't have to keep working at Sassy Seafood. Maybe there's another restaurant. One that only serves breakfast and lunch might be a better fit."

"Whenever I really check the hours, it's not good. Travis

and I have decided I'm going to have to quit working. Our son started acting up in school, and we both think it's because he's spending very little time with a parent. Any parent. Travis has been working long hours at his accounting firm, but he makes a lot more than I do in a restaurant."

"I know you have to decide what's best for you and your family, and every situation is different. If you could work part-time, but not in a restaurant's kitchen, would that interest you?"

"Only if the hours fit my schedule. I want to be here when it's time to send him to school and I want to be back when he comes home. If you have that perfect job, then I'm listening." Kelsey laughed.

"I don't know if it's perfect, Kelsey, but I'd like to hire somebody to help with my business. It wouldn't be fancy stuff. No more of the adrenaline rush of a restaurant kitchen."

"Or slicing and dicing for hours? Are you serious, Sam?"

"I am. My concern is if it turns out that my business can't afford you, then I would have to let you go. And that would really hurt, and I don't want to ruin our friendship."

Kelsey laughed. "This is fabulous. I can bring in some money and stay home with Oscar. Perfect, perfect, perfect."

Sam grinned. "You did hear the downside part of this, right?"

Kelsey laughed. "I did. The thing is that it gets me started on this new way of life. If it doesn't work out, that's okay, Sam, and that will not ruin our friendship. I'm hoping it does work out. What would you want me to do?"

"Pack up orders, help in the kitchen when it's production time, maybe interact with some customers online or on the phone. Does that sound appealing at all?"

Her friend giggled. "Yes. Thank you so much. When do I start?"

"I should be back in Anchorage next week. But I'm going to mail you the key to the storage area so you can ship a few orders this week. Is that okay?"

"Sure. Any word yet on your SUV and the damage?"

"Nothing. I called the mechanic a couple of days ago and he said he was getting to it. But Andy says he's the best, so I'll wait."

"And how are things with Andy?"

Sam grinned. "He's my host." But her heart said otherwise. She'd fallen for Andy O'Connell.

Sam's phone rang not long after she talked to Kelsey. She reached for it, hoping her friend had not changed her mind. Instead, the mechanic's number was on the screen.

Holding her breath, she answered the call. "This is Sam."

"Your vehicle is ready." The air whooshed out of her and then dread fell over her.

"What was the final cost?"

"The bill is actually less than I expected it to be. The job turned out simpler." Then he said, "Will you be able to pick it up today? I'm only here for another hour or so."

She checked the time. "Absolutely."

They hung up, and she ran over to Andy's door and pounded on it.

He opened the door. "What's wrong? Did something happen with the cats?" He looked around.

"My SUV's ready!"

"That's good." He seemed less enthusiastic than she'd thought he'd be.

"I don't have to be your houseguest anymore."

"That's true." Andy was acting strangely for a man who had not wanted anything more from her than friendship.

"He's closing soon. Would you be able to take me to get it right now?"

He moved into action. "Let's go."

As they backed out of the driveway with Gracie sitting between them, Andy asked, "Are you planning to leave tonight or are you going to wait until the morning?"

The daylight hours were getting longer and the days warmer, but there was still a fair amount of snow and ice on the roads. She much preferred not driving in the night in case she had an accident. Up until coming here, that had never actually happened, but her recent accident had made it all the more real. "I think I'll stay until the morning. Unless I'm imposing on you too much by doing that."

He shook his head. "No. Of course you're welcome to be here. Gracie gets one more night with her kittens."

Sam settled back into her seat as the conversation turned to another subject. "She does. She's going to miss them. Maybe I can bring her back to see the kittens in a few weeks. You know, before you give them away to new homes."

"That might not be the best plan."

She'd thought they'd built something while she'd been here. Maybe she *should* leave tonight.

When she stepped out of Andy's truck in the parking lot and had to grab ahold of the door because her foot slid, she decided to definitely wait till morning to leave.

Sam handed the mechanic her credit card, still in awe of

the low bill. And then it was her and Gracie back on the road again following Andy home.

Home.

Andy's house had become as much, if not greater, of a home than her apartment in Anchorage. She'd miss him and this place. That was certain.

The sun was setting as they pulled into Andy's driveway. She snapped Gracie's leash on. "Let's go take you for a walk before dinner." She lifted her down out of the truck and the two of them walked off. Maybe it would help Andy to have some time to himself.

He'd been a jerk. He'd only wanted to discourage anything that felt like a relationship, to act like a friend and nothing more. But instead, he'd come across as cold.

He had let Sam take over most of the cooking, but that and everything else in the house was going to be back on him, so he'd take that job back now. But his heart wasn't in it as much as it should have been. He decided to make a pasta sauce with some canned fire-roasted tomatoes, capers, and olives. He put water on for the pasta and continued his food prep.

Sam came in the door, glanced his way, and didn't even speak. She took off her coat and hung Gracie's leash up by the door where she'd been hanging it, but then she took it down and stuck it in her coat pocket. Must be in preparation for tomorrow so she wouldn't leave it behind.

In a small, un-Sam-like voice, she said, "That smells good." Then she added, "I think I'll let you cook and go pack everything so I'll be able to get out of here first thing in the morning."

She passed Jack in the hallway as he was coming out of his room. "I thought I heard some activity out there." He took one look at her expression and put his hands on her shoulders. "Sam, what's wrong?"

She felt tears welling in her eyes, but Samantha Santoro did not cry, especially not in front of others Swallowing hard, she said, "We just picked up my SUV. I'm leaving in the morning. Andy's making dinner if you'd like to go talk to him." She stepped back so his hands would drop away, and then she started down the hall.

"Sam, what's going on?"

She blinked a few times before turning back toward Jack. "I suggested I could bring Gracie back to see the kittens before Andy gave them away."

Jack shrugged. "That makes sense to me. That dog loves those kittens."

"Andy didn't want me to do that. I don't think I'll see you again, Jack. It's been a pleasure knowing . . ." She struggled with the rest of the words. "Knowing everyone in your family." Then she hurried down the hall to her bedroom and closed the door behind her.

Andy was stirring the sauce on the stove when he heard Jack bellow, "What have you done?"

He dropped the spoon and turned around to face his

older brother. "What are you talking about?" Guilt sank into him. He knew Jack must have talked to Sam.

"I'm talking about that woman who has been staying here. You know the one. The one you've fallen for."

Andy shook his head. "Absolutely not. She's a friend and nothing more. I don't want any complications in my life and that's the way it is."

"Can't you see what's in front of you? That woman is so in love with you. And you're going to throw that away for some relationship that ended long ago? One where the woman has moved on to the point that she is married and has given birth to a child?"

Andy stood firm. "It's my life and I can do whatever I want with it."

Jack shook his head. "Bro, you're going to regret this."

Would he?

When Andy watched Sam's vehicle drive away the next morning after only a few words spoken between them, he nearly called her back.

Jack stood beside him on the front step. "Still sure?"

He watched her taillights as she slowed down and applied the brakes to turn around the corner. "My decision stands."

When the SUV completely vanished, Andy started to wonder if he'd made the biggest mistake of his life. Should he chase her down?

No. He'd been right. Love hurt.

CHAPTER EIGHTEEN

*S*am got back to her normal life pretty quickly. At least, that was what she told herself every day during the first week. *Life was better than ever!* She kept repeating that, hoping it would finally be true. The truth of the matter was that she missed Andy.

In the middle of creating a new treat, one she thought Gracie would love, her phone rang. "Mom!" She did not feel like having this conversation right now, but she loved her mom. Sam sat on the couch and tried to relax. "How's everything with you?" Silence greeted her. She looked down at her phone, but it said the call was still there. "Mom, are you okay?" She was about to the point of hanging up and redialing when her mother spoke.

"Sam, what's wrong?"

She thought she'd done a convincing normal voice. Sam laughed, but that didn't sound right either. "Why do you think something is wrong? My business is doing better than ever." This time, she gave it even more enthusiasm.

"It's that man, isn't it? Andy. You haven't called since you returned home. All I got was a text that said your SUV was fixed, you were fine, and you were home. What happened?"

Tears filled her eyes. Sam had been battling this problem ever since she'd driven away from his house. She'd had to pull over in Soldotna so her vision could clear enough to drive.

Gracie snuggled up next to her and whimpered.

"I was a guest at Andy's house. Nothing more. Why would you think it was anything more?" There. She'd done a better job that time. The sentence had the right lilt at the end to make it sound like it was truly a question.

"Sam, please be honest with me. We've always been honest with each other, haven't we?"

They had. When her teenage friends had complained about their mothers being too nosy, she'd come home and discussed her dates with her mom. She'd always enjoyed talking to her. But this hurt too much. "Mom, I don't think I can talk about it yet."

In a softer voice, her mom said, "I can understand that, honey. You thought you had more between you than he did?"

Sam sniffed and held back the tears once again. "Yeah. But if you get me talking about this, I may start bawling like a two-year-old. I don't want to do that."

"You always were my strong one. Just know that I'm here for you. If you need me any time of the day or night, I'm here."

She sniffed again. "I know that, Mom. Thank you. Maybe he'll change his mind."

"I'm assuming this all ended the way it did because of his actions, not yours."

"I would say that you described it pretty well. When I was leaving, he made it clear we would not have any further contact. Not even for the kittens. And Gracie has been pacing around like you wouldn't believe since we got home. Boy, has she missed the kittens and maybe the cats too. I'm sure she misses those walks that she got to have in the wide-open spaces instead of next to the apartment in the tiny dog area."

"Maybe you should reach out to him. You could call first."

Could she? "Mom, when I picture his face that last day, I know that I cannot be the one to contact him. We'll hope that he decides I'm the one for him." This time the tears started running down her cheeks. She hiccuped. "Mom, I've got to go now."

"Take care of yourself, honey. And it's okay to cry sometimes."

Sam tossed her phone on the bed, flopped down beside it, and grabbed a wad of tissues. Gracie jumped up next to her.

"Us girls have to stick together, don't we?"

Gracie snuggled close to her and whimpered.

"I know. We both miss them."

"You are an idiot!" Andy stared at the face in front of him, his own image in his bathroom mirror. "You let her get away!" Was this the first sign of crazy when you started repri-manding yourself in your reflection? Must be pretty close. He braced his hands on the edge of the bathroom counter and leaned into it. "What have I done? I chased her away. Now how do I get her back?"

It had been two weeks since she left. The time was easily marked by the growth of the kittens. Today, they'd started playing. He'd thought about Sam and how much she would enjoy holding one of the kittens on her lap. And Gracie! She would be running around herding the kittens, making sure they stayed close to their mom.

He missed everything about Sam. Her looks. Her laugh. Her kiss. Just being with her whether they were cooking or hanging out in his living room. He missed her.

The first time he'd been rude and she'd driven away, she'd come back to him. This time, he didn't think he'd ever see her again. What was it about Sam that brought out such intense emotions?

He looked in the mirror again. "How do we fix this?"

At that, he turned away. He didn't want to have any actual conversations with his twin in the mirror.

Sam had come here for a website. She'd found him and his cats and new products for her business. And she'd left with a website that functioned.

He knew she wouldn't contact him and he missed her. He took a short video of the kittens as they stood on wobbly feet and he wrote a message, "The kittens are growing more every day." That should do it. It was appropriate for the situation. With his finger over the Send button, he hesitated. Before he could chicken out, he pushed it.

What was the situation? Stupid man lets a wonderful woman leave? Was there a greeting card with that sentiment on it?

A knock sounded on his front door. He hurried over to it, somehow expecting to see Sam there, but he only found his brother Jack.

"Oh, hey. What are you doing here?"

"It's good to see you too. I started looking around for a piece of photo equipment and finally figured out that I left it here in my room." He stopped and stared at Andy. "Have you changed your mind about going after Sam?"

Andy held up his phone. "I sent her a video of the kittens."

"That's a decent start. Did she reply?"

Andy's phone signaled an incoming text message. He looked at it. "She did." He didn't open it. What if she said not to message her again?

"Come on. I've never known you to run from something you wanted. Out of the five of us, you were often the one who chased after your dreams when the rest of us didn't. It took me years to figure things out. Not you. You were always good with computers. You knew that's what you did well and pursued it as a career." Jack stopped talking and stared at him. "Does your chasing Sam away have something to do with Lori?"

Andy froze. "Oh, my gosh!"

"What? It does? After all this time?"

Andy held up one hand in a stop motion. "I just realized that I haven't thought of Lori in weeks. Not once. All I think about is Sam."

"That is good. So are we going to go get her?"

Andy tapped his phone. "Step one of my plan was that I sent the video."

"And she said?"

Andy checked his phone. "'Thank you.'"

"That's all?"

"It isn't good. She signed it 'Samantha.'"

"That's her name, right?"

"The first day she was here, not long after she woke up, she said to call her Sam. That friends and family call her Sam. So, I'm no longer a friend." Andy waved his arms in frustration. "What do I do now?"

Jack pointed at his chest. "You're asking me? It took me forever to figure out that I loved Aimee."

"It took you a week alone. Sam's been gone for longer than that. I want her back. I want her in my life."

"Then go after her." Jack said each word deliberately.

"She lives hours away from here, and she has a life with the business she's been building for quite a while. That's where she needs to be." Andy heard his voice, but with its downtrodden tone, he barely recognized it.

"Sam needs to be wherever you are. Tell me the parts of her business you know about."

"She stores her treats in a storage unit. She planned to hire a friend to help with shipping. And she makes the treats in a commercial kitchen that she rents from a church."

"Okay. She needs a storage space. There are plenty of storage units near here."

Andy said, "I have so much room in my basement that I'm not even utilizing."

"Okay. Storage area solved. And what about this friend? Maybe the plan is that she can keep her friend on. Sam lives here and goes to Anchorage every couple of weeks. I know a commercial kitchen that's for sale not too far from here. She'd own her facility. Do you think she'd like that?"

"I know she would love that. The plan is that her friend continues to work for her, she can store things here if she wants to, and she can use a commercial kitchen down here. But I think the friend is supposed to help with that too."

"Bro, we're planning too much of her business. Give her a call and *talk* to her."

Andy jumped to his feet. "I can't do that. I shut things down between us when she left. I need to be subtle about this." He paced over to his windows overlooking the thawing lake and back to his brother. Then he turned and made the loop again. "I know! She needs her permanent website. She only has that temporary one I set up." Andy paused. "Unless she's contacted someone else to build it."

"Don't start second-guessing yourself, bro. Build her website."

Andy mulled that over. It made sense. "Okay, I'll get started on her website now. All of my rush jobs are complete, and I'm going to focus on that. I can have it done in a few days."

Jack clapped his brother on the shoulder. "Now you have a plan. And it's a good one. No one builds a better website than you do. If anyone can figure out a way to show love through one, it's you."

Sam wasn't sure what to do about the videos Andy had sent. When the first one came, she thought maybe he was just being nice. Because he was a very nice man who smiled a lot. He was one of those people you liked no matter what. Then the next day, another cute kitten video had arrived.

He'd started focusing on one kitten at a time and talking about what it liked and what it did. Every day for four days, she got a cameo of one of the kittens and its story. Then he sent photos of the kittens playing and some of his other cats. She even missed them. She'd gotten used to having a cat on the bed with her some nights. Gracie sometimes restlessly paced, and Sam knew she missed them too, since her dog had never done that before.

A week after the first video arrived, he sent her an email

with a link and the words, "It's a gift for you. Click the link, and let me know what you think."

Why was it that this man could make her cry when no other man had? Her mom would probably say it was because she loved this one, and she hadn't loved any other man. Sam clicked on the link, and it took her to her website. But not just any website. This one was amazing.

Jack had shot some photos of Gracie and the cats when she was there, and Andy had somehow turned them into caricatures. Not crazy cavorting ones, though. Gracie was at the top of the website next to her name. In the middle of the page sat Gracie and her crew of cats. As Sam flipped through the pages of the site, she knew that this was the most charming website she had ever seen. He'd spent many hours on it. That was clear.

After the initial look, she read through each page, one by one. He'd included all of her treats exactly as they'd done on the other website, but now it showed that the cat treats could be ordered for immediate shipment, not preorder. He must have been following her social media in order to know that. The Contact page looked good. She went to her About page. She'd flipped past it before, only noticing the cute photo of her and Gracie laughing. Now she stopped to read it.

Samantha Santoro loves cats and dogs. She loved her dog Gracie the moment she saw her in the shelter, and she named the business for her. But when Samantha was stranded at her friend Andy's house because of a car accident in the frozen Alaska winter, she discovered that she also loved cats. Goodness Gracie! began making dog and cat treats. All the treats have been taste tested by Gracie herself and Andy's four cats Lucy, Petunia, Kitty, and Happy.

When a cat treat was loved by some cats, but only so-so to another, Samantha kept working until they all gobbled it up. Oh, and the treats, of course, all passed Gracie's personal inspection. It was rather hard to stop a dog from eating a treat when it hit the floor.

Sam grinned at that. That was so true. Gracie still favored the turkey over the salmon, but she loved all of them.

Her customers would enjoy reading this personal story. It was kind of weird, though, that he'd included himself in it. She kept reading.

Andy fell for Sam when she was living at his house for that short time.

Sam gasped.

He loves everything about her and learned to love her dog as much as his cats do. But he was too stupid to realize it then. Now, he regrets any moment when he wasn't telling Samantha that she was beautiful and wonderful and that he loved her with every fiber of his being.

Andy wants to spend every day of his life with Sam. He hopes and prays she'll marry him.

Tears ran down Sam's cheeks, but this time, they were happy tears and she didn't try to stop them. She looked back at his original email, and now it made more sense.

"Gracie!" Her dog came running. "We're driving to Andy's house." Her dog began dancing on her back feet. Sam didn't know if it was the enthusiasm in her voice or if her dog knew what "Andy's house" meant, but they were on their way. She threw things in an overnight bag, grabbed her laptop and some snacks for them along with Gracie's food, and they were out the door in minutes.

She called Kelsey right away. "I'm not going to be able to meet you over at the storage area for a couple of days. Can you handle things?"

"Of course. Please tell me that's because of something good, though. Not that you drove into another ditch."

Sam laughed. "Oh, it's good. Andy proposed to me on the About page of my website."

Kelsey squealed. "That's awesome. Don't worry about a thing, Sam. I've trained with you enough now that I can handle all of it while you're gone. Let me know what has been ordered and who to send it to. I'll take care of the rest."

Sam could do that. It was a wonderful thing that she could run a business from a laptop.

She struggled to keep to the speed limit and was grateful that in April all the roads were clear of snow and ice. They stopped for a couple of breaks on the way, but even Gracie seemed antsy to get right back in the SUV and head on down the road.

She wondered if she should call Jack so he could spend the night. She didn't want to cause his mother any concern. At the next stop, she found his number in her phone from when she'd sent him the grocery list. She called him and explained the situation. "Can you help?

He laughed. "Gladly. Do you mind if I bring Aimee along? She just finished making an intricate necklace for a customer, and I know she'd like to have a getaway. He's got three guest rooms."

She really wanted to be alone with Andy, but she knew that was not how the family worked. "Sure. But can you give me a couple of hours alone with him before you arrive?"

"Absolutely. Hey, are you going to make dinner?"

Sam laughed. "I'll see what I can do."

She set her phone down and kept going. A half hour later, she turned onto Andy's road. Everything looked so different now that all but a few piles of snow were gone. When she came to a stop in front of his house, she saw a changed view. What would be green grass was brown and dried up, but his house was still beautiful.

Andy would be inside. She hoped she hadn't wanted it so much that she'd imagined the About page. It had said exactly what she would have wanted it to say if she'd written it herself. No, it had come from Andy's heart, so it was better than anything she could have written herself.

She clipped on Gracie's leash. "Let's go, girl." She lifted her down, and Gracie led Sam right up to the front door. The dog didn't hesitate, but her human did. Maybe she should call him first.

No, she'd come all this way.

As she held her hand in the air, the door opened.

Andy wrapped his arms around her and hugged her. "When you didn't reply, I thought you didn't care."

"Never think that. I care so much that I wanted to be here in person."

He leaned back so that he could look into her eyes. "Sam, can you ever forgive me?"

"You were forgiven as soon as you apologized."

He pulled her inside. Sam stepped through the door and dropped Gracie's leash. Her dog ran over to Lucy, Kitty, and Happy, and they touched noses like old friends. Then Gracie turned toward the hallway. "Andy! Stop her. She doesn't know how to act around the kittens!" They trailed after Gracie and found her sitting and watching the kittens play. One of them toddled over to her and sat on her foot. Gracie nuzzled it with her nose, and both seemed happy.

Andy put his hands on Sam's shoulders. "Sam, is there some way we can make this work? Your life is in Anchorage. My life is here. If I need to, I can move."

She could tell how much pain those words caused him. "Andy, this is a house I'd be happy to live in. Believe me when I say that this is far nicer than the apartment I have. Gracie loves it here, and I love it here. I'm sure I can make my business work. I'll need to go into Anchorage every once in a while to check on things, but I think I can handle the rest of it from here. And maybe Kelsey can come down sometimes to help too."

"I know someone who can get you on a good deal on flights from Kenai to Anchorage." He grinned.

For a second, Sam was confused, and then she grinned. "Oh, Noah."

"Sam, I need you in my life forever. Please tell me that you'll be mine."

She leaned forward and kissed him. "It's you and me forever." Gracie woofed, and Sam laughed. "And Gracie and the cats."

*S*am laughed as baby Clara ran across the grass as fast as her chubby legs would carry her. Mrs. O'Connell scooped her up and held her close, the little girl squealing and kissing her grandmother on the cheek.

Mark and Maddie had thought they'd miss Jack and Aimee's wedding the previous September, but she'd delivered Clara, the first baby in this generation of O'Connell's, a month early.

Sam lumbered to her feet and put her hand on her lower back. "I need to check on the food we brought. It must be time to eat soon."

Andy laughed. "Don't worry. They won't start eating without you."

She patted her belly. "I know it's cliché, but I'm eating for three. And these two boys are saying it's time for lunch."

Andy leaned down and kissed Sam. "How are you feeling?"

"Great!" She added extra enthusiasm to the word.

He cocked an eyebrow.

She sighed. "A little tired, but I'm going to give birth to twins in a couple of weeks. I am happy to be at the O'Connell family summer picnic, though, and glad to see Holly's sisters Jemma and Bree here too."

"I'll take care of the food we brought. Sit and relax."

"I think walking and standing are preferable to the picnic table's wooden seat." She rubbed her back again.

"I could bring over a lawn chair."

She laughed. "Andy, I'd be there forever because I'd never be able to get up. No. I need to waddle over to see your mom."

He grinned and held out his arm for her. "I'll escort you over there."

She put her arm through his. "I get along fine with your mom. Now. You don't have to be there." His mother sat watching her granddaughter, so they headed that direction. "Once we sorted out our differences—"

"You mean, once she forgave us for running away to Idaho to get married with your family in attendance, but not hers? She seemed to blame you for leading me astray." He added, "Dad wasn't too happy about that either."

Sam chuckled. "Your mother had her hand in the other weddings. Besides, we didn't plan to get married then. I remember standing in my brother's backyard on our trip to meet my family and mentioning that Idaho didn't have a waiting period to get married. The next thing I knew, I was in a little chapel—an adorable chapel—and saying 'I do.'"

He stopped walking and turned to face her. "You don't regret that decision, do you, Sam?"

She put her hand on his cheek and leaned close, as close as she could at least, and said, "Don't ever think that. I loved you then and I love you now." She put her hand in his and continued forward. "Besides, you mother quickly forgave us."

"Even though she did make the occasional comment about not getting to be at our wedding."

"Then all was forgiven." Sam paused to rest. "The moment we announced I was pregnant, she stopped mentioning it. I know she loves me, but it was nice to be back in her good graces."

Rachel walked over. "I haven't gotten to talk to you lately, Sam. How is Goodness Gracie! doing?"

Happiness rushed through her. "It's going so well! Business is booming with dog *and* cat treats."

"And Gracie and the cats?"

Andy answered. "Everyone's happy. And the kitten we kept isn't so small anymore. You need to visit again. She and Gracie are inseparable."

"We love Pumpkin, the orange kitten we got from the litter. Are you going to have time to keep your business once the boys are born?" Rachel had a concerned expression. "I've wondered about running a business with a baby."

"Kelsey is working out well and I may hire another employee too. Having help seems to be the key." Sam realized that this wasn't only about her. "Rachel?"

Her friend blushed at the unspoken question. She leaned forward and whispered, "Noah and I decided to wait to share the news until after we knew if it was a boy or girl. We found out yesterday." Rachel giggled.

Aimee and Jack joined them. "Is this a new party?"

Sam put her hand on her belly. "It may be the world's shortest party. I'm going to need to sit soon."

Jack smiled at his wife. "Let's all go over to Mom and Dad. We have news to share."

Sam gasped. "Not you too?"

Jack glanced around the group and stopped on Rachel. "More babies?"

Rachel nodded. "Mrs. O'Connell kept saying she wanted her sons to give her grandchildren."

Aimee grinned. "She has said that many times. I don't think she's going to say it again."

Sam started for the picnic bench nearest her in-laws. "Let's all sit down. I'm glad our stories turned out so well. Next Christmas will be filled with babies and laughter. And Gracie and the cats."

WHAT'S NEXT?

Each of the O'Connell brothers meet their match in the Alaska Matchmakers Romance series. But matchmakers Jemma, Bree, and Holly met their husbands in the Alaska Dream Romance series. If you haven't read them yet, you don't want to miss *Falling for Alaska* (Jemma's story), *Loving Alaska* (Bree's story), and *Crazy About Alaska*, (Holly and Adam's story).

Also,

There's a FREE, short story tied to these books. Pete and Cathy are in *Falling for Alaska*. Pete—Nathaniel's lawyer—and Cathy—a woman on a hike with Jemma—are minor characters, but their cute first meeting is a FREE short story. I liked them so much that I brought them back in *Crazy About Alaska*. Get your FREE short story by going to cathrynbrown.com/together.

ABOUT CATHRYN

Writing books that are fun and touch your heart

Even though Cathryn Brown always loved to read, she didn't plan to be a writer. She earned two degrees from the University of Alaska, one in journalism/public communications, but didn't become a journalist.

Years passed. Cathryn felt pulled into a writing life, testing her wings with a novel and moving on to articles. She's now an award-winning journalist who has sold hundreds articles to local, national, and regional publications.

The Feather Chase, written as Shannon L. Brown, was her first published book and begins the Crime-Solving Cousins Mystery series. The eight-to-twelve-year-olds in your life will enjoy this contemporary twist on a Nancy Drew–type mystery.

Cathryn enjoys hiking, sometimes while dictating a book. She also unwinds by baking and reading. She lives in Tennessee with her professor husband and adorable calico cat.

Made in the USA
Columbia, SC
12 November 2022

71072087R00117